WES HARDIN'S GUN

WES HARDIN'S GUN

JOHN REESE

DOUBLEDAY & COMPANY, INC.

GARDEN CITY, NEW YORK

1975

All of the characters in this book are purely fictional, and any resemblance to actual persons, living or dead, is coincidental.

Library of Congress Cataloging in Publication Data

Reese, John.
  Wes Hardin's gun.

  I. Title.
PZ4.R3294We [PS3568.E42] 813'.5'4
ISBN 0-385-08897-3
Library of Congress Catalog Card Number 75-3644

Dedicated to the staff at the
Santa Maria Public Library

WES HARDIN'S GUN

CHAPTER ONE

The train clanked northward into the lengthening shadows of a January day, the engine running easily ahead of a dozen empty boxcars, a gang car, and a caboose. The gang car was an old boxcar in which two windows had been installed in each side. Coal smoke poured from a stovepipe in the roof. The freight doors had been removed, and smaller doors installed in each side, near the iron ladders at each end of the car.

Inside the gang car, a tall, brawny young man walked in his sock feet to the nearest window and looked out. From his left wrist dangled a pair of handcuffs. He wore only a dark flannel shirt and worn Levi pants. The dim light from the window showed a controlled, impassive, fair-skinned face with small blue eyes. His hair had been recently cut short. He had a month's growth of pale, silky beard that made him look both a little biblical and a little wild.

He opened the door of the potbellied stove quietly, with the coal shovel. He threw several lumps of coal into the fire, from a box against the wall. He used his left hand, holding the dangling handcuff with his right so it would not clatter against the stove.

Two men lay in the bunks that lined the walls in the front end of the car. One slept on his back, arms folded under his head, using a sheepskin coat as a pillow. He was short, wiry of build, gray-haired, and with a seamed, mean-looking face. On his vest he wore a badge engraved with the word, SHERIFF.

Across from him, the man slept on his face with his hat covering his head, and wearing his coat. He was about midway between the sheriff and the handcuffed youth in size. Now and then he shivered violently in his sleep.

The youth tried to close the door of the stove silently, but it slipped, and the door clanged loudly. The man sleeping on his stomach turned on his side and pushed away the hat that covered his head.

"Al," he said, in a hoarse voice, "you're about as housebroken as a bull buffalo."

"What happen, I burn my son-of-bitching hand," the youth apologized, with a strong German accent.

The sheriff opened his eyes too. "Mr. Hewitt," he said, "you don't look so good."

"I don't feel so good," said Jefferson Hewitt. "I think it's settling into my chest. How long before we get to School Hill?"

Sheriff Art Gavin sat up. "If we don't have to switch at the siding—say, two hours. But if we do, it could take an hour to thaw out the switchpoints."

Hewitt shuddered with a strong chill. "I wish I had a stiff drink."

"Maybe they've got one in the caboose."

"Not if Red Cameron is on the division, they won't."

"Who is Red Cameron?"

"Don't you know Red? He's a Burlington special agent, and he's hell on the rule book."

"Well," the sheriff said, "it'd be a strange boomer crew that wasn't prepared for snakebite. Al, lean out the door and catch the lookout's eye. See if they ain't got a bottle back there, for a drink for Mr. Hewitt."

Hewitt sat up and saw the dangling handcuff for the first

time. "Sheriff Gavin, if you don't mind the comment, that's a hell of a way to secure a prisoner."

Gavin's mean little face creased in a smile. "Your company is going to bail him out anyway. Why should I handcuff him?"

"*If* a judge admits him to bail, and *if* the money is wired to School Hill on time. And if we ever get there."

"I knowed Albrecht Raue since his family first came here, Mr. Hewitt. He's a good boy, and he turned himself in, like you promised. Now, if you want him cuffed, you say so."

Hewitt stood up, a man of average height, perhaps forty years old. His face was plain, with a strong chin, a firm mouth, deep-set, hazel eyes, well-cut brown hair and a stiff, short brown mustache. Under his Mackinaw coat he wore a shirt of white wool, a beaded deerskin vest, and a black tie held by a pearl stickpin.

"He's your prisoner, Sheriff. I imagine you know what you're doing."

"Sometimes I do. Albrecht, do like I said. See if that crew has got any snakebite medicine."

The youth held up the arm with the handcuff. "They can't hear me from the door. Take this off, and I'll go back and ask them."

The sheriff tossed his key ring across the car. "The shortest one. No, turn it to the left, dummie!"

"It ain't all the time I'm wearing handcuffs, Art. I'll practice yet," said Albrecht Raue.

He dropped the handcuffs and tossed the keys back to the sheriff. He stepped into his boots and opened the door in the rear corner of the car and leaned out. A gust of icy wind chilled the car quickly. Hewitt began shivering again, as he saw Raue lean out, grasp the iron ladder, and swing outside. He went to the door, closed it, and returned to stand close to the stove.

"I like that kid, Mr. Gavin," he said, when the shivering fit had subsided.

The sheriff said quietly, "He didn't kill that feller, Mr. Hewitt. Al is the least quarrelsome kid I know. There may be some in School Hill that'd like to see him come back in chains, but I run this job to suit my own self. And he ain't going back handcuffed."

"I have heard about you, yes I have," Hewitt said.

"Oh? What have you heard?"

"Oh . . . that you fought with Sheridan. That you have been married to the same woman for forty years. That you play a middling poor hand of poker, but make up for it with the way you handle a gun."

The sheriff nodded. "I ain't a trick shot, like they say you are, but I don't mind the reputation. If people believe that of you, they ain't so apt to make you prove it."

"My own theory! I won't bet I can make any given shot, but I won't bet I can't, either. But right now, a kid with a bean blower could take me."

Several sharp thuds sounded on the rear of the car. The sheriff jumped to his feet. "Stay out of the draft, Mr. Hewitt. That's Al, throwing coal at us. I hope he got a bottle. You sure don't look good."

He opened the door. The prisoner half stepped, half fell into the car. In his hand was a square brown bottle that had held a quart. It was about half full. He carried it to Hewitt, who had sat down on his bunk again.

"They thought I was escaping," he said. "I ain't even got a gun, and they was scared to death! It sure got to be funny."

"I can see where you might laugh yourself to death that way," Hewitt said. "Thanks, Al. Here's how!"

It was not very good whiskey, but it helped. Gavin refused a drink, and Hewitt did not offer the prisoner one. He corked the bottle and put it on his bunk.

"Put the cuffs on again, Al. One wrist," the sheriff said.

Raue grumbled, but he obeyed. Hewitt lay back, trying not to smile at the picture the youth made as he earnestly locked the handcuff around his own wrist. The whiskey gave a little respite from the fever and chills. In a moment, Hewitt got up and went to the window—the one on the left as he faced the front of the train.

It was almost dark. This was rough country, with the low hills that went under the name of "mountains" here. The Black Hills were not far to the north, nor the sandhills of Nebraska far to the south. Everywhere he saw small trees, but the outcroppings of rock betrayed the shallowness of the topsoil. Still, between the trees, the hills and the rocks, there were fields of wild bluestem grass—the richest kind of feed, and lots of it.

A few of these "parks," as they were called, had been plowed and planted to oats or barley. Only stubble remained now, but a heavy crop had been taken out this year.

The sheriff came up behind him. "These old Nebraska hills ain't the richest country in the world, but me and my wife wouldn't live nowhere else," he murmured.

"Yes. We seem to be slowing down, Sheriff."

"Siding is just ahead. They have to take on water before they switch. Whoever put the water tower out here wasn't thinking, seems to me."

"I guess you drill for water where it is."

"Then why don't you build the siding where the water is? It's a mile away."

The clank of couplers losing slack echoed through the car. Hewitt had to steady himself by holding to the nearest bunk, but he noticed that young Raue had the sense of balance of a cat. He did not even take his hands out of his pockets, as the freight train stopped.

They were on a curve that turned sharply to the right. From where Hewitt stood, he could see only more of the same—small trees, hills, and grassy parks.

"Not much snow so far," he murmured.

"No, and there'll be no spring grass unless we get some soon," said Gavin.

Movement caught Hewitt's eyes among the trees. He wiped the window with his sleeve, and then could make out horses standing bunched under the trees. No free horse would stand like that, so close to a train. He looked for the shapes of men.

He saw them, several of them on the ground, and he did not know why he felt suddenly uneasy. Was it the fever and chills, and the lightheadedness that went with them? He looked around and saw Albrecht Raue opening a lantern to light it.

"Don't make a light in here!" he said sharply. "Sheriff, come here."

Gavin came to the window. "Mighty strange," he murmured. "Only time this siding is used is when somebody is shipping cattle. This time of year, the siding is just dead storage, both tracks. How many men do you make it?"

"I would say five."

"I wonder if it's the State Line Gang?"

"What's that?"

"Oh, bunch of rowdies up around the South Dakota border. Just grocery-store robbers, but they killed a man and they beat an old couple half to death."

"I am always uneasy when I've got a prisoner."

"Me too, Mr. Hewitt. I ask myself, now why are they freezing their hind ends out there this time of night? Can you still see what they're doing?"

The light was fading fast. "Yes. They're leading their horses back, away from the train. No, just one is. Now he's mounting up. He's leading the other four. He'll cross the tracks behind us."

"What the hell! I don't like this."

"Neither do I." Hewitt crossed the car to the other window. He could see almost the whole train now, on the wide curve. The engine had stopped at the ice-crusted water tower, where steam leaked from the pump house. The fireman was on top of the tender, holding the big spout that gushed water into the tank. It looked like the coldest job in the world.

Beyond the pump house was a section house, and some grounded boxcars that had been turned into houses for section hands. No other human being was in sight, but lights twinkled in the modest homes under the trees. The tiny depot was dark, but beyond it, Hewitt could see two endless rows of boxcars and slatted livestock cars, in dead winter storage on two side tracks.

The fireman pulled the lanyard to close the valve. He swung the spout up and away from the engine, and jumped down into the warm cab. A brakeman came out from between two cars of the train, and swung his lantern. The engineer replied with a hoot of the whistle. The train began moving.

I wish I had a clearer head, Hewitt thought. I don't know what I'm getting into, and I can't think. . . . He unbuttoned his Mackinaw and felt the .45 that lay in a holster he had designed himself. It clipped to the belt that held his pants, with the butt tilted for easy access, the front sight locked under a pawl. A sharp twist freed it, and it was the readiest holster he had ever used.

He had only to shrug his left arm to know that the .38 was in his shoulder holster. He heard the sheriff, behind him, take out his .45 and spin the cylinder. So it was not just fever. Gavin was worried, too.

"He's going to tie on the other side of the boxcars on the side track," the sheriff said. "There's another one, on foot. That'll be two on the west side of the tracks, Mr. Hewitt. What do you make of it?"

"And three on the east side," Hewitt said. "It looks like a stick-up, to me."

Albrecht Raue chuckled. "Holting up a freight? What can you steal from a freight train?"

"You," Gavin said softly.

"Me? What they want with me?"

The sheriff snarled, "Hang you, what the hell else? Al, no matter what happens, don't try to run for it. If they get you afoot in this weather, at night, you're a dead man. But by God, kid—when I get you to School Hill, I bet I find out what you been up to!"

"I ain't been up to nothing!"

"Then why do they want to hang you?"

"Who said they want to hang me? That's crazy, Art. Why does anybody want to hang me? I don't do nothing to damn nobody!"

There was bewilderment in the kid's voice, but no fear. Hewitt took the .38 out of his shoulder holster, and caught Gavin's eye with a questioning look. The sheriff nodded. Hewitt held the gun out to the kid.

"Put this in your pocket. You can't waste lead. My ammunition is all in my suitcase. Don't lose your head, now. Do as the sheriff says! We won't let them take you."

"Why they want to take me?"

"I don't know. Maybe they don't. Let's check the bet now. See what happens."

Hewitt stood back from the window as the train crept around the curve. The pump house slid past, and then the lamplighted crew houses. Suddenly, everything was blotted out by the two rows of stored cars on the side tracks.

The train stopped. The engine whistled a reply to a brakie's signal.

Then the engine went chuffing off, taking most of the train with it. Hewitt could make out only two boxcars left ahead of the gang car. For a moment, the only sound was the wail of the cold wind in the stovepipe. Then he heard the sheriff breathing behind him.

"What now, Mr. Hewitt?"

"The horses will be tied beyond the side tracks, Sheriff. The three that were left on the other side of the tracks, I'll bet, rode the ladders this far. They'll come at us from both sides."

"It's the State Line Gang, but what the *hell* do they want with Al? It beats me."

Movement caught Hewitt's eye—the peak of an old hat, as someone ran past the window between the gang car and the stored boxcars on the side tracks. He heard the grating scream of rusty iron, and recognized the sound of a boxcar door being forced open.

Then a slug ripped through the window on the other side of the car. The window disintegrated, showering the car with glass. Another slug ripped through it and buried itself in the roof of the car.

"Al! Stay near the center of the car," Hewitt said softly. "They're not going to hit anything shooting from down on the ground."

A moment of silence. Then—

"Hey, inside there!" a voice called. "You hear me, Sheriff Gavin?"

"Don't nobody answer," the sheriff whispered. "Let the sons of bitches guess."

Another brief silence. Then, two more shots that angled up through the pine siding of the car, and into the roof. "Sheriff, we ain't funning," came the same voice. "Come out with your hands up, and you won't be hurt. All we want is that backshooting Dutch kid."

Another chill suddenly shook Hewitt. He snatched the bottle up out of his bunk and gulped twice. Too much of this stuff could floor him, but the need now was to stop shaking. He replaced the bottle and then leaned over to touch Gavin on the arm.

"Sheriff, listen. There will be at least one man with the engine crew. That leaves four for here, two on each side. See that open door in the car opposite us? There'll be a man or two in that car, what'll you bet?"

"You're prob'ly right."

"The firing will all come from the other side, to drive us out this side. The minute we do, they'll cut us down from inside that car. How much of a ride would it be for Al Raue to School Hill on a good horse?"

"He could make it by morning, but—"

"Their horses look like good ones. There's a coal scuttle by the stove, and a two-gallon can of coal oil in the coal box. Suppose you watch on your side, and I start smoking the open door of that boxcar. I can make it hot enough to keep anybody back from that door.

"Let Al take a scuttle full of burning coal from the stove and the coal oil can. Throw both into that car, and then just duck under it and watch his chance to go for the horses. Let me get into my suitcase for bullets, and you and I can stand them off here until doomsday."

You didn't need a hammer to pound sense into this old sheriff's head. "Yes. We can fort up here forever, once Al is gone and they're afoot."

"They won't be afoot. They'll take the engine."

"But they won't have my prisoner." Gavin motioned Raue to them. "Al, listen to Mr. Hewitt. We're going to learn these bastards a thing or two about lynch law."

Hewitt explained what they expected of Raue. "Oh sure, I could do it, but I fight mine own fights," Al said. "Thanks, Mr. Hewitt, but I stay here."

"You do as you're told. Leave coals enough to start the fire again, that's all. Throw your oil in first, then your fire, and then duck under the car. When the fire blazes up, go for the horses. Grab one, turn the others loose, and ride for School Hill. Now go!"

Several more shots ripped into the roof, as Raue filled the coal scuttle with fire from the stove. The same voice demanded the German youth's surrender.

"Ready when you are," Raue whispered coolly.

The sheriff could do nothing but fire slowly and blindly through the shattered window on his side. Hewitt held his fire until Raue opened the door and dropped to the ground. The big German kid was quite cool, as he took his scuttle of blazing coals and the can of coal oil, and vanished from Hewitt's sight.

Hewitt pumped one . . . two . . . three shots into the half-open door of the freight car opposite. Raue loomed up below him in the darkness. Hewitt fired once more, just as Raue swung the coal oil can around his head and smashed it down on the floor of the boxcar—hard. Hewitt could see the bright drops fly in all directions.

Raue swung the scuttle of coals into the car and dropped to his knees. A man with a heavy black beard loomed in the door, just as the oil blazed up. He had a gun in his hand, and the nerve to jump the sea of fire that had suddenly engulfed the car.

They shot at the same time. Hewitt heard the man's slug shriek past his ear, and then the scream ripped from the throat of the bearded man as he twisted and fell on his side in the fire.

Another man appeared briefly in the car, with a shotgun

gripped in his left hand. The fiercely blazing oil and coal illuminated the horror on his face, as he saw he had no chance to
jump the fire. Hewitt could have pitied him, except for that
shotgun. They would have cut Raue down like a mad dog.

The boxcar was afire everywhere. Someone was shrieking
hoarsely inside it, louder than the roar of the flames. A horse
screamed, too, and then Hewitt heard Raue shouting, "Hyah,
hyah, hyah!" Someone fired twice, on Gavin's side of the
car, but the sheriff was standing in the center of the car,
calmly reloading his gun.

"Reckon Al got away," he said.

"I think so," Hewitt replied. He leaned against the nearest
bunk, thinking, I'm going to have another shaking fit. I can't
hold onto my gun. Damn it, I wish I could stop shaking. . . .

Sheriff Art Gavin's mean little face swam before his eyes.
Somebody had him under the arms. Somebody else was picking up his feet. Someone was stoking the fire in the stove in
the center of the car.

"Lay down and take it easy, Mr. Hewitt," Gavin was saying. "The engine's gone. We're plumb out of targets."

CHAPTER TWO

Hewitt supposed he slept an hour. Another chill had hold of him. He groped in the bunk for the bottle, pulled the cork with his teeth, and got down another drink. He managed to sit up, and in a minute was able to stop shivering and try to think.

Someone had hung sacking over the shattered windows. Louder than the roar of the fire in the stove was the mad howl of the one consuming the boxcar. Hewitt stood up and stumbled to the window. He pulled the sacking aside, and felt the heat on his face.

The roof of the car had collapsed. The floor, made of two-inch hard pine, was a mass of fire. Below Hewitt, men ran past carrying buckets, but they did not empty them on the fire. They were trying to keep the nearby cars wet enough to save them.

At every country depot stood two barrels of brine that would not freeze in the coldest weather. Over each hung two conical buckets that could not possibly be used for anything else, since they would not stand by themselves. Thus, they were always there when they were needed to fight fire.

The train and section crews had long since run out of brine. They were now trotting back and forth to the section foreman's well. About all they had to do now was wait for the fire to burn itself out.

The door opened and Gavin climbed in. "You rest, Mr. Hewitt," he said. "This car ain't going to burn."

"Did Al get away?" Hewitt's voice was a croak.

"Yes."

"How about the gang?"

"There was five. Two burned up in the car. One put a gun on the engine crew, and he picked up the other two before they went helling south again. Mr. Hewitt, nobody seen them hanging around here today. Nobody recognized them. That engine has to go to School Hill. We'd have them by the tail, if I could get word there."

"Can't you wire somebody?"

"There's no telegrapher here. Anyway, they pulled the wires down."

"I can send, if we can splice the lines."

"Mr. Hewitt, you haven't got no business going out in this cold. It's four below zero on the thermometer on the depot wall. There's nothing we can do."

Hewitt said hoarsely, "I'm good for a while yet. The engine will get to School Hill long before Raue. What'll they do there? No point in getting Al out of here, if he's waylaid there. Let's give it a try, Sheriff."

Every country depot had a roll of wire, for the use of signalmen repairing storm damage. Hewitt had no way of knowing which of the two lines was the company wire, and which the commercial. They spliced both. The section boss had no key to the depot. He broke the window, crawled inside, and unlocked the door.

The instruments were already clicking, proving that the lines were now clear. Hewitt could not find the operator's code book, to look up the School Hill signal. He could only break in and demand the wire:

EMERGENCY EMERGENCY CALLING SCHOOL HILL COME IN SCHOOL HILL FOR IMPORTANT EMERGENCY CALL

The moment he closed his key, the wire answered. He had to break in to tell the operator to slow down. He transcribed as it came in, Gavin leaning over his shoulder to read:

THIS IS SCHOOL HILL WHO ARE YOU QMK PLS IDENTIFY

Hewitt had to translate this. "QMK" meant "question mark," "PLS" meant "please." He tapped out an answer, reading aloud to Gavin as he sent it:

AMATEUR OPR OFF TRAIN 2145 STOP TRAIN HELD UP STOP ENGINE CREW MISSING STOP HEADED YOUR WAY STOP SHD ARRV SOON STOP SHERIFF GAVIN ORDERS DEPUTY HUTTON TAKE MEASURES ACCORDINGLY STOP WHEN ALBRECHT RAUE ARRIVES HE IS NOT REPEAT NOT A FUGITIVE STOP THIS IS IMPORTANT

School Hill replied promptly:

ENGINE ALREADY SIGHTED NEAR LANSING XING STOP HUTTON ON WAY STOP HOW AND WHEN EXPECT RAUE QMK

At Gavin's orders, Hewitt replied:

RAUE ARRV DAYLIGHT HORSEBACK STOP WARN HUTTON THREE MEN ON ENGINE ARMED AND VERY REPEAT VERY DANGEROUS STOP KEEP US INFORMED

Now there was nothing to do but wait. Men came in to report that the fire was out, with no serious damage to any other cars. The burned car was still too hot for them to try to recover the bodies of the dead men, but it was clear that they were burned beyond recognition.

The men drifted out, leaving Hewitt and Gavin alone in the office, where someone had started a fire in the stove.

"Mr. Hewitt," Gavin said, "I'm afeared we've lost again. Lansing's Crossing is a good two miles from town, up on a hill. This time of night, you could easy see the headlights of an engine. What worries me, Porter Lansing has good horses, lots and lots of them. They'll help themselves, and be long gone by now."

"Who is Porter Lansing?"

"Banker. It was his bank where this feller was killed that Albrecht Raue was supposed to've murdered. Porter's an old-timer. God knows how much he's worth." Gavin chuckled. "You know what his favorite possession is? Wes Hardin's gun!"

"The Texas outlaw?"

"Yes. Porter paid a hundred and fifty dollars for that forty-five Hardin used to tote, after he died. Keeps it in a velvet-lined box. I bet he takes a lot less pride in it after he loses three high-priced horses to these killers. All that outlaw excitement ain't so much fun, when you're the victim."

Hewitt tried to smile. "No indeed! I knew Wes Hardin—at least I met him, right after he got out of the Texas pen."

"Oh? How'd that happen?"

"I wanted to see if he could help us on a case I was working. The man I thought I wanted had been in the pen at the same time as Hardin."

"Did he?"

"Oh, he talked freely enough, but he was no help. I think his mind was gone. John Wesley Hardin had guts, no denying that. But I think he killed more men than any of the old gunmen, and I never did know one of those fellows who wasn't a little loony."

Unexpectedly, the sheriff put out a callused hand, laying the palm on Hewitt's cheek. "You're hotter than the hubs of

hell, you know that? You've got a real bad fever. You ought
to lay down and try to sleep."

"Wait a minute—here's a call for us."

There was almost no night traffic on either wire, and one
of the sounders was clicking away:

FIRST REPORT ON ENGINE STOP ENGINEER MURDERED
FIREMAN REPORTS THREE MEN DETRAINED LANSING XING
STOP THEY PULLED ENGINE FIRE STOP NEED HOUR GET
STEAM UP THEN WILL RETURN TO PICK UP YOUR TRAIN
STOP HUTTON IS PURSUING STOP DOES SHERIFF WANT
DESCRIPTION FUGITIVES NOW QMK

"Tell them," Gavin said, "to write it down before they forget it, but don't bother us with is now. You're pretty good
with that there telegraph, Mr. Hewitt."

Hewitt transmitted the sheriff's message. "It's one of the
things I had to learn. I live by the telegraph. I—I think I
would like to flop down now, Sheriff."

They had to help him back to the gang car. It was midnight before the engine reappeared. The jolt as it coupled to
the train awakened Hewitt, who found Gavin watching him
soberly, when he sat up.

"I hope there's a good doctor in your town, Sheriff," he
said.

"There is. Young German by the name of Ernest Schickel.
You feel like talking?"

"Sure. What about?"

"Seems you're going to a lot of trouble, in a case where
you know you won't be paid."

"Well, that's the way this business goes. You clear your
conscience this way, so you can demand a bigger fee on the
next case."

"Mind telling me your interest in Albrecht Raue?"

"My partner is a German immigrant, too. I'll try to clear Raue, if he's innocent. If he's not, my partner will just have to get used to it. From what you say, they can't convict him anyway."

"*Clearing* a man is a lot different than just *not convicting* him in a small town."

"I see."

Gavin sighed. "Burden of proof is on the prosecution, sure. And they can't prove that Albrecht killed that man. But if Al means to spend the rest of his life around here, and he has any regard for the family name, he's in trouble. That kind of talk can foller you for the rest of your life."

It was Hewitt's turn to sigh. "Only way to clear a man beyond all doubt is to convict the man who is really guilty."

"In a small town, especially."

"I've had cases like this before."

"Ever have one where you wreck a whole goddam town, while you're saving one innocent man?"

Hewitt studied him a long time. "I wish I knew exactly what you mean by that, Sheriff."

Gavin looked down at the floor. "I hope I'm wrong. Well, you go back to sleep, Mr. Hewitt. We'll be there soon enough. This is a mixed-up case, but it'll still be there when you're well again."

There were few kinds of cases that Jefferson Hewitt had not experienced, human nature being the repetitive thing it is. If his years as a private detective had taught him nothing else, it had convinced him of the truth of the Old Testament saying that there was nothing new under the sun.

It was almost twenty-five years since a boy of fifteen came out of the Ozarks, barefoot, barely able to read and write. His name was not Jefferson Hewitt, then. He lied about his age to join the Army, where immediately he felt he had found a home.

The Army system, that put a stout fence between enlisted men and officers, did not bother him. What did was the superior education, knowledge and manners of most officers. The boy who then was Hugh Goff had only one talent. Luckily for him, it was one that the Army valued. He was a crack shot with both the long gun and the short. A silent, watchful youth, eager to learn and willing to work and able to shoot, did well in the Army.

He never rose beyond the rank of corporal, but as company clerk, he had discovered (with some wonderment) the deep-seated fear most people had of making decisions. Having no such fear himself, and having to make decisions for his officers, gave him a self-esteem that was new to him. It taught him to look for other talents in himself, to encourage and develop them.

Today, Jefferson Hewitt had the wide knowledge and the self-assurance of a self-educated man who could hold his own in any company. He spoke several languages adequately, one or two fluently, one or two passably. He was good at identifying regional accents, and after a few moments' talk with a stranger could tell him where he came from within a few miles. He knew music well enough to enjoy it, without playing it. He could have made his living as a portrait artist in charcoal or crayons, as gambler, masseur, livestock broker, mechanic or woodcarver. He knew more law than many a lawyer.

And today he was an even better marksman. Over the years, he had seen to it that his reputation exceeded even his abilities. He could throw a knife, if he had to, and he always carried a shot-filled, leather sap. This "cosh," as outlaws called it, was a much-neglected weapon, Hewitt felt. The sap had saved him many a dangerous fight with guns, knives, or fists.

Hewitt was a private detective because that was the first job he found after leaving the Army. He had made his reputation with the Pinkerton agency, running down a runaway boy heir, freeing a rich man's son of the suspicion of murder, and winning a rich settlement from a husband who had his eye on a younger woman. He had worked divorce cases—thefts from companies—thefts *by* companies. One mining company and one bank that had tried to take a man's ranch away from him were among the "respectable" companies that had discovered that Hewitt could be as dirty as he had to be, to win a case for a client.

Hewitt was at his best in land, cattle and horse cases. He could rough it as long as he had to, going dirty, sleepless and unshaven to make his case, but he liked good clothes, good hotels, good food and pretty women—and the big fees that put such good things within reach.

He had long ago learned that there were usually both wrong and right on both sides—that few losers were ever really reconciled to losing—and that few winners were ever as grateful as they had promised to be. On the wall of his office in Cheyenne (which he saw rarely) hung a little framed motto a client had given him. It said:

THE UNDERTAKER'S CODE
If you would succeed in this gentle, tender calling,
Be sure you strike your deal while the tears are falling.

He had worked under many names, changing personality as he changed names. "Jefferson Hewitt" was now his "real" name, because he liked this personality better than the others.

After a few years with Pinkerton, a Wyoming bank had

offered to back a partnership between him and Conrad
Meuse, a German immigrant, and the best accountant Hewitt
had ever known. Bankers Bonding & Indemnity Company
was an equal partnership. Meuse ran the Cheyenne office,
writing surety bonds for corporation and public officials.
Hewitt did the field work.

It was said that only the very rich could afford B.B. & I. In
a sense, this was true. Conrad grumbled when Hewitt turned
down a fat fee, because he did not like the smell of a case. He
grumbled even more when Hewitt spent time doing jobs for
clients who could not even pay expense money.

Yet Conrad always paid his share of these costs. They
were not just partners—they were friends, despite the fact that
they could not stand each other's company for very long at a
time. Hewitt always dreaded the quarrels over his expense accounts—and it was not just the principle of the thing that
made them quarrel. The money mattered.

Conrad invested Hewitt's money for him. He had made
Hewitt a wealthy man. Neither had retired, for the same two
reasons. Both were restless bachelors to whom work was an
addiction. And both were avaricious. To fight for principle—to take risks—to defend the right because it *was* right—
ah, that was fine! But it was still finer, with a healthy cash
fee riding on success.

Hewitt liked women. Conrad thought of him as a predator
who was eternally stalking some woman at the partnership's
expense. It did not happen as often as Conrad thought. But
there had been enough such cases to give Hewitt a guilty feeling, so that he was vulnerable when Conrad wanted free serv-
ice for one of his German friends.

Hewitt had been finishing a case in New Mexico, when a
letter from Conrad caught up with him. It urged Hewitt to
hurry to School Hill, Nebraska, to clear one Albrecht Raue
of a murder charge. There would, Conrad said, be no fee.

But he did not see how Hewitt, with his lifelong passion for justice, and so on and so forth, and his brilliance and skill, and so on and so forth, could refuse so pitiful a case. Then Conrad had continued:

We still have not reached agreement on the $750 fee to Mrs. Rose Locke. A lot of money, my friend Jefferson! My correspondents disclose that Mrs. Locke is a very pretty young widow, and that she wept and then fainted as your train pulled out. This does not seem like the behavior of one who has truly *earned* $750. But we will say no more, once you have cleared Albrecht Raue of the charge of murder.

Hewitt still would have liked to know who Conrad's correspondents were, but he knew it was useless to ask. All he could do was proceed to School Hill, and charge it off to some delightful memories. That Rose—ah, what a woman!

CHAPTER THREE

Hewitt was not really conscious when they took him off the train in School Hill, and he was lucid only now and then for the rest of the night, the next day, and most of the next night. Several times, he was aware that he was in a warm bed, and that a woman was bending over him, in a gentle but firm voice urging him to stay covered.

She was a very pretty woman, with streaks of gray in the braids piled in a stately coil on top of her head. She made him drink water. She washed his face and hands. She wiped his forehead and temples with cologne.

A man who was surely a doctor drifted in and out of his delirium. The worst part of it was that Hewitt knew he was delirious, but the shapeless terrors were somehow worse for knowing that. He was a man who hated to lose control of himself in any way, but the fever was too strong for him.

And then suddenly he was wide awake on his back in bed. He was drenched with sweat under a mound of heavy blankets, and he could feel a hot-water bottle at his feet and another on his stomach. He was too weak to sit up, but he could look around.

He was in a double bed in a small, neat room in which a lamp burned low on a small bureau that was the only other piece of furniture. Besides the lamp, the bureau also held medicines, wash cloths, a pitcher, and a basin. By craning his neck a little, he could see his suitcase, open on the floor beside the bureau.

He drifted off to sleep, forcing the Raue case out of his mind. First things came first, and the job now was to get his strength back.

It was still night when he awakened again. He found that if he took it slowly, he could sit up and swing his feet out of bed. There was a braided rug under them. The door was half open. Hewitt was in his underwear. His face was covered with stiff beard.

And he was suddenly so hungry that it was a real pain in his stomach. He managed to stand up, but his knees betrayed him and he sat heavily down again. The noise the bed made embarrassed him.

He heard someone coming. The woman with the gray-streaked hair was in the doorway, closing a flannel wrapper around herself. Her feet were bare, and very pretty feet they were, he thought.

"You're better," she said. She was prettier than he had thought, when she smiled.

He tried to smile back, and it was a relief to be able to talk without croaking. "Yes. Fever's down. I get sick fast, but I get over it fast, too."

"You can't get out of bed yet. I'll bring a chair for you, while I change your bed."

Before he could object, she brought a straight kitchen chair and helped him into it. Since she was not embarrassed by his underwear, neither was he. She stripped the bed with housewifely skill and brought fresh sheets.

"You'll feel better in clean bedding. You have clean night-shirts, too, you know."

"I would like a bath first," he said.

"Not until the doctor says so."

"Then how about a cigar?"

She finished the bed and took hold of his arm to help him to it. "No cigars, Mr. Hewitt. Doctor's orders."

"Then how about a cigarette?"

"You have no paper or tobacco."

"I'm as good as dead, then."

She laughed. "I'll bring you the makin's. If you're able to roll one, I'm sure the doctor would say you're well enough to smoke it."

Halfway through rolling the cigarette, his hand shook and tore the paper. She rolled one for him, deftly, and then one for herself. She held a match over the lamp until it ignited and lighted both their cigarettes.

While she was bringing a saucer from the kitchen for an ash tray, he remembered something from his delirium—what Sheriff Art Gavin had said. "You're Mrs. Mystic," he said, when she returned. "Gavin told them to take me to Miz Mystic's place, I remember that."

"No, I'm Mrs. McDonald. Mystic is my first name."

"And a very pretty one, too."

"No, merely foolish. I'm one of those dreary widow-women who remember so many foolish things."

"Let me guess. Vermont? But you have lived in the deep South, too."

It took her by surprise. "You're uncanny, sir. It was New Hampshire, but Father bought a business in Macon when I was ten. I lived there until I married and came here to School Hill."

"Accents are a hobby of mine, Mrs. McDonald."

"Please don't call me that. Nor 'Miz Mystic,' either. It's so long since I've talked to anyone about anything but bank, church, and school, I should like to be plain Mystic to you."

"Thank you for that. I'm Jeff to my friends. You work in the bank?"

She seemed to hesitate. "I'm supervising bookkeeper, but that's only a few hours a week. I'm on the board of directors, too. My husband was cashier and vice president."

"Which bank, may I ask?"

She smiled. "Not the one you're interested in, the German one. I'm with Farmers and Merchants."

"That would be Porter Lansing's bank."

"Yes. I have been saving some broth for you. It's frozen on the back porch. While I'm heating some, you put on a fresh nightshirt. Plenty of time to talk business later."

She went out, closing the door. He got into the nightshirt before she returned with the broth. She held the broth while he spooned it up. As he ate, she told him all that had happened while he was ill.

The three fugitives on the locomotive had killed the engineer with his own hammer, when he tried to pass the Lansing ranch. They had then forced the fireman to shake the grates, dumping his fire on the tracks, and then open the blowoff cocks to drop his steam pressure. The gang had put a gun on Porter Lansing's foreman, and then had helped themselves to three of Porter Lansing's best horses. When last seen, they were riding north.

"Bayard Hutton—he's Art Gavin's deputy—went after them with three men. There still has been no snow, and it was almost impossible to track them. The three men came back just this past evening, half frozen. Bayard still hasn't given up, and Isobel—that's his wife—is frantic with worry."

Albrecht Raue had arrived in School Hill before daylight. At eight, a telegraphic money order for two thousand dollars had come from Bankers Bonding & Indemnity Company, and at ten, Judge Burt Williams had admitted Raue to bail in that amount. Raue was now working for a German cattleman southwest of town, not far from Porter Lansing's ranch.

"What about the horse Raue rode?" Hewitt asked.

"That's interesting, Art Gavin says. It's a good one, with two white stockings that had been blacked out with stove polish. The brand is a strange one. Art thinks it's Mexican, a big, wavering line down the hip, with some curlicue cross-marks. There's some sort of Spanish name for it, Art says," Mystic McDonald reported.

"*Rúbrica* is the word," said Hewitt.

"You speak Spanish, do you?"

"A little." (In fact, Hewitt spoke it fluently.) "The *rúbrica* goes back to before the time when cattlemen were expected to read and write. A *rúbrica* was both a legal signature and a livestock brand."

She nodded, showing interest. "You were talking some foreign language in your delirium, Jeff. I studied French once, and I've heard enough German to recognize it, but it was neither. Italian, perhaps?"

"Probably." He finished the soup. "I wonder if I could have another cigarette?"

"That sounds nice!"

This time, he rolled his own and she rolled hers. They smoked in silence a moment, he feeling a fool in his night-shirt on the edge of the bed, with his bare feet on the rug, she on the straight chair just inside the door.

Suddenly she stood up. "It's almost four. Dr. Schickel would scold me in two languages, if he knew I had let you stay up this long," she said. "But I'm so glad you're better."

"A sick man is at the mercy of strangers. I was lucky."

She touched his shoulder lightly with the tips of her fingers and went out, leaving the door open. One of those women who become not just pretty, but beautiful, as you get to know them. Not a frontier type. His own age at least, and not at all embarrassed by having cared for him during his illness. Poised, worldly, and, he thought, more than a little lonely in this isolated town.

He did not expect to sleep; but he did.

He got up and dressed the next day, but it was two more

days before he ventured out on the street. No one came to see him. Mystic McDonald was absent from the house most of the day, and not communicative when she was at home.

The house was a small one, but it had the best view in town. From the parlor, which was closed off in the winter, Hewitt could look down the hill and see all of the town. Mrs. McDonald's bedroom opened on the parlor. Behind these two rooms was a dining room, and then a small, neat kitchen. Hewitt's room was an afterthought, built on behind the kitchen.

Mrs. McDonald saw him start down the hill path with some concern, and she persuaded him to pick up a piece of brushwood for a staff. He was soon glad that he had taken her advice, because even with the help of the staff, his legs were shaking by the time he reached the town.

The path came out in a wide alley behind the Farmers and Merchants Bank. He circled the building. Between it and a law office next door, there was a wide empty space. Mystic had pointed it out from her window. This, she said, was where the body of the man Albrecht Raue had been accused of killing had been found.

"Do you think Raue killed him?" Hewitt had asked her.

"I have no way of making a judgment. Dick is the man who identified Raue. We don't see many Germans in our bank," she replied.

"Dick" was Richard Lansing, son of the president of the bank. From a number of sources, Hewitt had learned that Dick was in his middle forties, unmarried, and not quite worthless. He drank too much, had no real responsibility in the bank, and was liked without being respected.

The bank wall, on this side, was part wood siding and part stone masonry. The stone, of course, housed a built-in safe or vault. Hewitt had been in enough rural banks to know that most of them took better precautions against burglary than city banks. The vault would be lined with three-quarter-inch armor plate, and the massive steel door with its combination lock would be welded to the plate.

There was a deep gouge in a board under the single small window on this side. This, no doubt, was where Art Gavin had cut out the .22 bullet that had killed the man. That small window was the one where Dick Lansing was supposed to have seen Al Raue, not long before the estimated time of the murder.

Hewitt had to step up almost a foot to the limestone sidewalk. The town was bigger than it looked from Mystic's house. One block to the south, and across the street, stood the American Eagle Bank—the German bank, which was bonded by B.B. & I. of Cheyenne. Time enough to visit them when he had his strength back, and a better sense of direction in this stale old case. Otto Groshardt, president of the American Eagle, was the man who had called Conrad Meuse into the case.

Hewitt rested a moment, leaning on his staff, and then started across the street toward Junkins' Saloon, from which came an appetizing odor of steak frying. He was halfway across when he heard the ring of a shod hoof on rock. He turned and saw a bay trotting stallion come out of a cross street, pulling a racing sulky driven by a tall old man in a black cowhide overcoat, with a Scotch cap pulled down over his ears.

The horse was getting a real workout. Hewitt knew who the man was instantly, and he knew that the horse was heading straight at him. Had he felt confident of his legs, he could have jumped for it.

His hand slid under his coat and came out with his .45. He could only hope that his hand was steady enough to impress Porter Lansing.

It was the horse that flinched, breaking gait, not the driver.

The old man hauled him in with an expression of surprise that did not fool Hewitt a bit. Hewitt holstered the gun and went to the side of the sulky.

"I'll bet this horse is O'Malley's Leo, and you're Mr. Porter Lansing," he said. He did not offer his hand.

Lansing stepped down from the sulky but did offer his. Hewitt took it. "And you'll be Mr. Hewitt, the detective," Lansing said. "I wondered why you didn't jump lively, but you've been sick, haven't you?"

"Do you usually run people down this way?"

Lansing roared with laughter. "Well, I'm blind as a bat when I'm working a good horse, and folks know that and kind of put up with a foolish old man. Horses are my passion. We've had miserable goddam horseflesh in this country. I've brought in the best, Mr. Hewitt. I tell you, long after my bank is forgotten, my goddam horses will be a monument."

They measured each other. Hewitt was familiar with the type—old cattleman turned banker because it was the only way—or at least the fastest way—to bring a bank to a growing community. It always turned out to be richer than ranching, but most of these tough old pioneer bankers never lost their range-bull toughness of body, mind, and speech.

Porter Lansing was at least seventy, but he carried the years lightly on a frame at least six feet three. Hard blue eyes, big chin, long upper lip, good teeth in a mouth as straight and hard as an ax-mark in oak. And he means to find out, right now, if I can be bullied, Hewitt thought. Well, let's try him on. . . .

"O'Malley's Leo—isn't this the horse that was mixed up in the murder, Mr. Lansing?"

"They never proved it on him." Again that loud, crude guffaw of laughter.

"What's he worth now?"

"I overpaid Jim Sweetland for him, but I wouldn't take

twice that for him now. I've got sixteen mares in foal by him. I'll found a race of fine horses on him."

"You've heard no more from Sweetland?"

"Nary a word."

"It's queer."

Lansing lowered his voice. "Mr. Hewitt, this used to be a good town to live in. A good town to do business in. People was happy here. That's all gone to hell, but what worries me, you might make things even worse than they are."

"Murder never does a town any good."

Lansing said explosively, "It wasn't the murder. It was long before that! It's that goddam German bank. I was the best friend the Germans ever had. Germans are good farmers, good stockmen, good merchants—and lord, how we needed good farmers and stockmen and merchants! But look around you. Do you see business enough for two banks in a town this size?"

"I'm not the best judge of that."

"The hell you're not! You bonded Otto Groshardt, didn't you?"

"I believe we did."

"You know damn well you did! When they finally close up, where'll that leave you?"

"Unless there's embezzlement, we won't be hurt. We don't guarantee that a bank can make money—only that we'll cover losses by criminality within the bank."

"They can hurt me—yes. They've already done that. But you mark my words, Mr. Hewitt, someday I'll take over that bank's assets, and Otto can go to work for me or go back to farming."

"Do you mind saying who is on your own bond?"

"You know the answer to that, too—J.I.B.C. Mr. Hewitt, do you take me for a damn fool? I know a lot about you, and I know that you know a hell of a lot more about me. Now, you go ahead and try to prove that Raue kid didn't kill that man, if you like—"

"Do you think he did?"

"Yes, but that's Art Gavin's business, not mine. Only thing I want to say is, don't poke your nose into what don't concern you. Do your job, but don't make things any worse than they are. Because if you do, it might make things worse for you, too."

"Mr. Lansing, are you threatening me?"

Lansing pounded him roughly on the back, and roared with laughter. "Mr. Hewitt, when I threaten a man, I make damn sure I can make good on it. I don't think I'd care to tangle with you, sir."

O'Malley's Leo was getting restless. Hewitt helped Lansing into the sulky again, and watched him drive the fine trotter on down the street. If he had learned nothing from Lansing, he was fairly sure that Lansing had learned nothing from him.

And that was exactly why the old man had tried to run him down this morning, using the same brutal fun with which rowdy cowboys made things miserable for the townsmen. Jump out of the way, or take the consequences! Well, Hewitt thought, we'll have to look into his bonds a little . . .

J.I.B.C. was Jersey Interstate Bonding Corporation, a big, old, rich company. Its management had grown old, and too conservative. J.I.B.C. had been slow to venture into the West. When it did, it took so long on its investigations that many a bank opening was delayed a year or more. A few never did open. J.I.B.C. simply did not know how to make judgments on rough-and-ready cattlemen who wanted to open banks.

And this was the reason that Jefferson Hewitt and Conrad Meuse had been able to open their own firm. A growing country could not wait.

Hewitt ate his first full meal in Junkins' Saloon and enjoyed every bite of it. He knew that every man in the place knew who he was, and that not all of them were happy to see him there. Lansing was right about one thing—this was a sick town, as infected with suspicion as Hewitt himself had been with the fever a few days ago.

He was just starting up the hill when Mystic McDonald caught up with him. She had on an old coat, but she wore a bright red tam-o'-shanter that made her look like a schoolgirl. She took his arm and insisted on steadying him, as he toiled up the hill. And what a womanly way she had about her, to do it without making him feel a fool!

Hewitt opened the door and stood aside for her to enter. She still had hold of his arm. She dropped her hand to take his, and he held on until he had closed the door behind him. He brought her hand up to his lips, and kissed her mittened knuckles lightly.

Her eyes danced; and when she smiled, two unexpected dimples showed. "You're very sure of yourself, Mr. Hewitt, aren't you?" she said.

He got her meaning. "No," he said, "but there are times when I wish I were."

CHAPTER FOUR

Hewitt took a long nap that afternoon, and when he awakened, was ravenously hungry. He also felt better than he had in two weeks. Mystic McDonald fried ham and made sandwiches and coffee for him. Hewitt had barely finished when Sheriff Art Gavin appeared.

With him was a huge, lumbering man with red hair going gray, and a hard face that wore a perpetual snarl. Red Cameron, the Burlington special agent, towered over the little sheriff by more than a foot. He and Hewitt respected each other, but they were not friends, and their handshake was brief and almost violent.

"Heard you was up and about. I let you alone long as I could, because the way I size things up, there's a harder trail ahead than there is behind," Gavin said.

Mystic opened the parlor and touched off the fire that was laid in the stove. She put another pot of coffee on, and made Cameron at home with housewifely courtesy. Red and Gavin both refused food. When she went out to bring the coffee, she closed the parlor door behind her.

"You always light on your feet, don't you, Jeff?" Cameron said.

"I'm not sure I know what you mean," Hewitt replied.

"Why, you ain't done a day's work on the case, and you're already fixed up like the Duke of Connaught. Never seen a nicer house or a prettier woman."

Hewitt said calmly, "Well, I'll tell you how that is, Voyle.

Live like a gentleman, and oftener than not, you'll be treated like a gentleman."

Cameron winced as though from a blow to the belly. He hated his first name, which Hewitt had been saving for just such an occasion as this for years. Art Gavin could barely conceal his glee. There was no question in Hewitt's mind but that the sheriff both respected and liked Mystic McDonald and had resented the inference against her.

"Reckon you're right," Cameron said. "What I want to know is how the hell you figure the State Line Gang is in this case of yours. They been nothing but trouble to us. Now they've cost us a boxcar—or you have, since you figgered out how to set fire to it."

"Is it definitely the State Line Gang?"

"Pretty sure. One of that gang is supposed to have a little limp. One of the men burned up in that box car had a short leg, the doctor says."

"Red, I had never heard of the State Line Gang until Sheriff Gavin mentioned it."

Cameron squinted at him. "There'll be a reward out for the other three that killed our engineer."

"How much?"

Cameron shrugged. "How much would it take to interest you?"

"I'm on another case."

"One that won't pay one dime."

"You know how we work. I couldn't leave it to work for you for a fifty-thousand-dollar reward."

"How about sixty thousand?"

Hewitt smiled. "Keep talking."

The railroad dick laughed and slapped Hewitt's knee. "All I'm saying, Jeff, is this: Looks like your case is mixed up with the State Line Gang. If we can work together, the Burlington will make it worth your while."

"Sure, Red, we've got to work together."

"And we won't hurt your feelings a bit if we offer you a little fee when it's over?"

"I say praise the Lord for small blessings, and large ones in proportion."

Cameron stood up. "I'll leave you now. Got a few things to do. Just like to say I'm glad to let bygones be bygones. And please thank the lady for her very kind hospitality, will you?"

He let himself out, and they could see him going down the path, a big bull of a man who was always in a hurry.

"How far can you trust him?" Gavin asked.

Hewitt held his hand up, thumb and forefinger a quarter of an inch apart. "About that far, unless you know him."

"And you do."

"Yes."

"You've had trouble with him."

"Sheriff, you don't really know Red Cameron until you've had trouble with him. I'll tell you this much, I feel better to have him on our side. If Red could control his temper a little better, there might be the best law enforcement officer in the world."

"We can use that kind of help. My deputy got back last evening. I wish he had a little brains to go with his guts. He was close enough to them fellers to worry them. They went almost to the line, and then circled back in this direction."

"Your deputy is sure?"

"He says he is, and he was on their tails long enough to know their tracks like you know the palm of your hand. I know one thing. With them back in this country, I'd feel better if we had Al Raue in jail."

"It's an idea."

They talked over the case. Hewitt had run Raue down, where he was working for a cattleman near Alliance, Nebraska, before getting in touch with Gavin. He had then sent

Gavin a lengthy telegram, offering Raue's surrender if he would come to Alliance to discuss the case first. The two men had met at the Alliance depot, Gavin full of suspicion, and frank to say that he did not care much for private detectives.

"I've always tried to help that kid. I doubt they can convict him, but when he runs off like he did, what's a man to think?" he demanded.

"He didn't run off, Sheriff. He didn't even know he was wanted, until I told him. He swears he hasn't been in School Hill since April, and I think we have witnesses who will testify that he never left this area."

"Hell, you can find witnesses for anything! I've got one who testifies, under oath, that he seen him in School Hill on the sixteenth of September."

"If he's an honest man, then it's a case of mistaken identity. Sheriff, I *think* Raue is going to go back with you peaceably, if he's not frightened first. But he's just a kid, and he's upset at being suspected of murder. My worry is that he's going to spook and run for it. I hope we can come to an agreement that—"

"I don't do business with middlemen. You tell me where he is, and I guarantee he'll go back, and I fu'ther guarantee he'll get a fair trial."

Hewitt had had to make up his mind fast. This Gavin was by no stretch of the imagination a charmer. He was, in fact, an easy man to dislike. But the Germans who had supplied Conrad Meuse with information had said he was both brave and honest.

"That's exactly the kind of deal I want, Mr. Gavin."

"Don't make no mistake! If Al killed that man, and I can prove it, he'll either hang or go to the pen."

"I can shake hands on that."

Thus began the train ride back toward School Hill, with Hewitt already coming down with what he thought was only a cold. He had not seen anything to decrease his trust in, and liking for, Sheriff Gavin.

Albrecht Raue was accused of having shot, from ambush, a stranger in the wide alley beside the Farmers and Merchants Bank, at about three-fifty in the afternoon of September sixteenth. Dick Lansing swore that he had looked out of the little window behind the teller's cage a few minutes after three. He was sure of the time, because he had come through that same alley a few minutes before, and had been at his father's desk at three.

Besides, a fall thunderstorm was brewing, after a hot, dry summer. And Hewitt knew that people's impressions were sharper under such circumstances. You could believe a man who said he kept track of the time, with a storm coming on. Also, lightning made Dick Lansing nervous, and everyone remembered the hard, bright, vivid lightning that was flashing then. It was one such flash that had so brightly illuminated the man he saw in the alley.

But the body was not discovered until the next morning. The dead man had been about thirty years old, five-ten in height, and one-fifty in weight. Brown hair and eyes, month's growth of brown beard, brown hair uncut for several months. He wore badly worn range clothing, but his hat was a peaked Mexican *sombrero* that had cost at least twenty dollars not long back. In the pocket of his pants was a sealed letter that said:

Porter Lansing, Esq.

The bearer brings $500 to apply on my note. Will pay off the bal. before March, then I want to buy back O'Malley's Leo. Hope your price will be fair, and think I am entitled to that. In other words, don't try to hold me up.

Yrs. sincerely,

Jas. E. Sweetland

Jim Sweetland had been a small rancher who went broke trying to be a big speculator in fine horses. Gavin described him as being a moody, quarrelsome old bachelor with few friends. Porter Lansing's bank had foreclosed his mortgage a year and a half earlier. Lansing himself had bid in Sweetland's prize sire, O'Malley's Leo for $1,250. It had been, at the time, a breathtaking record price.

But Sweetland himself had quietly vanished from School Hill. No one had heard from him—or of him. Porter Lansing said that Sweetland had no note at the bank.

"How could he? He had no credit," Lansing had told Sheriff Gavin. "I let him have about eleven hundred dollars of my own money, over a period of about two years. I never expected to get it back. You have to do these things every now and then, and I've taken bigger losses than this. If Jim sent me any money, I'd appreciate it. But I'd be surprised as hell, too."

There was not a cent in the dead man's pocket. He carried no other papers. His horse, if he had one, could not be found. Gavin could not find anyone who had seen the man in town. The body remained on display for three days, and no one recognized it.

"I figger he came in on a freight train that got in about five after three," Gavin told Hewitt. "With that storm coming on, he could've hiked up back alleys from the tracks to the bank, and no one might see him. But there ain't many bums and boomers riding the freights lately."

Not with Red Cameron working the division, Hewitt agreed. Any trainman who let a man ride free risked his job these days.

Dr. Ernest Schickel's autopsy showed that the man had been shot in the head from behind, at pointblank range, with a .22 bullet that probably had been fired from a rifle. It had passed all the way through the head, to lodge in the wood siding of the bank. Gavin had the bullet with him, and he showed it to Hewitt. It had been badly distorted by its triple impact—twice through the dead man's cranium and once when it struck the wood.

"Here's what I want to know, Mr. Hewitt: How do you slip up behind a man in broad daylight, carrying a rifle, if that man is already so spooky he's sliding up alleys to get where he's going?" Gavin asked.

"I know what I would suspect," Hewitt replied. "The dead man and the killer were a team—at least friends. They arrived together, and this was the murderer's last chance to make off with the five hundred dollars."

"My own idee. Ain't a bit strange that nobody heard a twenty-two. They don't make much noise, and it was thundering to beat hell. I just wonder, though, why Dick Lansing seen only *one* man in the alley."

"A man I think we can prove wasn't within a hundred miles of here. How good a witness is young Lansing? Is he a drunk?"

"He admits to me that he had a couple of drinks, because he was going in to have a showdown with old Porter about something. Dick is a kind of a queer drinker. One drink makes him red-faced and sweaty. Two, and he'll talk your arm off. But after that, he'll put away a dozen without them showing."

"Then he's a drunk."

"I reckon. This is only a personal judgment, but I think that Dick thinks he's telling the truth. I know for a fact that he's always been friends with Al Raue. And Dick keeps saying that he only said he *seen* Al in the alley—not that he seen him shoot anybody. And I tell you this much, Mr. Hewitt—maybe Al could get mad enough to shoot somebody in a face-to-face fight. But from behind? No!"

"Yet Al owns a twenty-two rifle."

"Yes. I rode out to his folks' place and picked it up. They

claim they hadn't seen Al in months. They said the gun was took out and used twice, to fire at coyotes that was in their chicken yard. The rest of the time, it hung in a sort of kitchen closet."

Hewitt would never forget taking Gavin out to the ranch near Alliance to arrest Raue. The kid was furious. "I ain't going back by this kind goddam foolishness," he said. "Go ahead, shoot me. But I ain't going."

"I ain't going to shoot you," Gavin said. "I'm just going to kick your hind end all the way to School Hill. Now, you cut this out and give me that gun."

Unexpectedly, the kid looked at Gavin and broke into laughter. He unbuckled his gun belt and handed it over. "All right, you pay my ticket. I been thinking I'd mebbe go home anyway." He looked at Hewitt, still grinning. "A man gets homesick, you know?"

"I know," Hewitt said. "You like School Hill?"

"Sure, don't you?"

"I've never been there."

"Well, you watch out for the sheriff there. That Gavin, he's a mean old bastard."

Hewitt could not help smiling. "Some sheriffs I know, you could be spitting out teeth for a week, talking about them that way."

"And I'm one of them," said Gavin.

"You see, don't I tell you?" said Raue. "He's a mean old bastard."

It was almost impossible to think of this joking kid as an ambush murderer, but Hewitt had met a few murderers in his time. Not all of them looked and acted the part.

"I wonder what Lansing would say if I asked to examine the bank inside," said Hewitt.

"What do you expect to learn there?" said Gavin.

"I don't know. Probably nothing."

"We can go find out."

Hewitt looked at his watch. "Too late today, isn't it? I've got five-fifteen."

"Porter never leaves until six or six-thirty."

"It must be pretty dark by the time he gets out to his ranch."

"He don't go out there very often. Porter's got a house here in town. He keeps a housekeeper since his wife died. Just him and Dick live there. I think that's why he works so late in the bank. Lonesome."

Mystic McDonald heard them at the front door, and came from the back of the house to ask if Hewitt would be back soon for supper. She seemed not at all concerned over having it known that he was still a guest in her house, but Gavin was distinctly not at ease.

"I'm not hungry, ma'am, so you had best not wait for me. Tomorrow, I'll look for a room elsewhere," Hewitt said.

"There isn't much to look for, as Art will tell you. I wish you'd stay here, Mr. Hewitt."

He thanked her with a nod, a smile. Going down the hill, it was Gavin who broke the silence. "She's right about one thing. They ain't a decent place to stay in this town. Across from the depot is the Railroad Saloon. It's got rooms for rent upstairs. That's where the commercial travelers stay, but you couldn't expect a decent woman to stay there, and a man could get sick of it mighty fast."

"Let's lay our cards on the table, Sheriff. I like Mrs. McDonald and I like my room at her place, but I wouldn't want to stay at the expense of her good name."

"She ain't got any. Mystic does as she damn pleases, always has, always will. People kind of quit talking about her because nobody could ever *prove* anything. And when you come right down to it, there wasn't nothing to prove, prob'ly."

"I see."

"I doubt it. Anything good that happens in this town, you'll generally find Mystic behind it—Mystic and the women she keeps stirrin' up. Know about her husband?"

"Only that he was an officer in the bank."

"He ran off with another woman, and took eight thousand dollars of bank money with him. Mystic had a little money she inherited from her family. She paid off the bank, but she gave old Porter Lansing hell for letting it happen. Said he wasn't worth a damn as a banker, she could do a better job herself, made them elect her a director.

"Porter says Mystic gets more done in a few hours than his other help done in a week, before she set up a new book-keeping system. People may not *like* Mystic in this town, Mr. Hewitt. But they listen to her. She's the brains of that bank."

"What happened to the husband?"

"Took aconite poison when he ran out of money and the woman left him. Tell you something else, Mr. Hewitt, that not everybody else knows. McDonald owned some stock in the bank—about ten per cent of it. One of the reasons he skipped, the bank wasn't making money and that stock wasn't worth a damn. Mystic inherited it—or you might say she paid for it by paying off his embezzlement. But today, from what I hear, that stock is worth a lot of money."

They were at the bank. A curtain was drawn over the small, barred window in the heavy front door, but Gavin pounded on the door until Porter Lansing came to open it. The banker looked annoyed at first, but his strong, ugly face broke into a grin when he recognized Hewitt.

"Just thinking about you, Mr. Hewitt, and wishing we could have a drink together. I hear you're a crack pistol shot," he said.

"It's part of the trade I follow," Hewitt admitted.

"Then you may be interested in a gun I own. It cost me a

hundred and fifty dollars, and it used to belong to John Wesley Hardin. Ever hear of him?"

"Yes. I met him, in fact."

"You did? When?"

"After he got out of the pen. Not long before he was gunned down."

"Now by God, we've got to talk about that one of these days. Come here, I want you to see his forty-five. They say Hardin killed forty men before he was twenty-one. Supposed to have killed the first six or seven with this gun. I've made a study of his life. It was a great waste, Mr. Hewitt, because Hardin could have been a great man at everything he did. What a pity life forced him into outlawry!"

Hardin's gun was a sentimental treasure to the old man, whatever its market value. He unlocked his desk and took it out, an ancient Navy Colt .45 with worn walnut butt plates. Hewitt examined it carefully.

"What do you know about the history of this gun?" he asked the banker.

"Hardin got hard up and pawned it with a friend, and the friend hid it and was afraid to own up he had it because just about then, Hardin became wanted by every lawman in Texas. Few years later, the friend gave it back to Hardin. I bought it from a man who got it from a woman by the name of Ruby Coll, some kind of lady friend of Hardin's."

"I know Ruby Coll. I told Sheriff Gavin I wanted to see the inside of your bank, and he suggested that we come straight down. I'm sure it's inconvenient—"

"Not to me, but you won't see much in the dark," Lansing cut in. "Look around all you like, but better come back by daylight tomorrow."

"Not much use looking tonight. I wonder, though, if you would care to express an opinion on whether Albrecht Raue is guilty or not."

"Hell, I don't know many of those young Germans! I used to know all of the old-timers, but they wanted their own bank, and they got it."

Lansing carefully wrapped Hardin's gun in its wrapper of oiled cloth, and put it back in the drawer. After a thoughtful moment, he went on: "You mean because my son is a witness against him—is that why you wonder how I feel about the Raue kid?"

"More or less."

"Well, Mr. Hewitt, you'll hear many things to the discredit of Dick. Most of 'em will be true, but I reckon I'm not the first man to have a worthless son, and won't be the last. Dick wouldn't lie—I'll say that for him. But I don't know any more than you do about Albrecht Raue, and I ain't for or against him."

He slammed the drawer shut, turned the key in it, and shook the drawer to make sure it was locked.

"Like to set down and talk to you about Wes Hardin sometime. This country is going to hell, Mr. Hewitt, because the people are getting soft and worthless. If I'd had a son like John Wesley Hardin, I could've made something of him. A leader, instead of a killer. But Hardin got prison and then assassination, and what have I got for a son to hand everything I own to? A nice, pleasant little boy, sir—a forty-six-year-old little boy that can't carry his liquor. That's life for you, Mr. Hewitt."

CHAPTER FIVE

They parted in front of the bank. "Me and the wife want to have you over for supper some evening, but you look as tired as I feel," Sheriff Gavin said. "You still ain't a well man yet, Mr. Hewitt."

"I'm all right. I bounce back fast," said Hewitt.

"Wait till you're my age, and you won't. Go home and get some sleep. That's what I aim to do."

"That's the best idea yet."

Hewitt started slowly up the hill to Mystic's house, buttoning his Mackinaw about him closely. It was surely close to zero right now, he thought. He was used to working in any weather, but he did not like extreme cold, and—

A big man loomed up in front of him, hurrying down the hill. "Jeff! Miz McDonald said you'd went to the bank. I want you to come with me and see something," said Red Cameron.

There could have been a better time for it, Hewitt thought, but Red Cameron was a good man, and he would not waste their time. Hewitt turned and walked down to the depot with him, in silence. No use asking Red questions. He would talk when he was ready, not before.

On a set-off by the tracks stood a little three-wheeled hand-car just big enough for two men, the kind used by inspectors and servicemen. It had various names among railroaders, but the commonest was a "bug." Unlike the larger gang hand-cars, which were pumped with an up-and-down motion, this one had handlebars that were pumped horizontally. Two men could ride it, facing each other, both pumping.

Red unlocked the padlock with a standard Burlington switch key, picked up one end of the bug, and put it on the tracks easily. He pointed to the front seat, and Hewitt mounted it to ride backward. It felt good to be pumping vigorously in this cold, but Red's powerful arms did most of the work.

They headed south, outrunning the light, cold breeze. "I suppose it's a waste of time to remind you that we're breaking every rule in the books, by running without a lantern lighted," Hewitt said.

Red laughed his deep laugh. "No trains running tonight. Anything else gets in our way, it'll be sad for them."

More than a mile from School Hill, a steep grade began, and both men had to pump harder. They were nearing Lansing's Crossing, Hewitt knew, where the engine had been stopped and the engineer killed. Now Red Cameron began talking as he pumped.

"I had the division superintendent talk to all the trainmen who have run this line in the last few months. I got a long wire from him this afternoon, and caught the frieght out this far and walked the track myself. Had to walk back to town, and I ain't had supper yet. But by George, I think this may mean something!"

They pumped almost to the top of the grade, stopping where Hewitt could see, only a few hundred yards away, the glow of lighted windows at Porter Lansing's ranch. Cameron stopped pumping and got off.

"Let's be quiet now. I have to kind of feel my way in the dark. I wish we'd thought to bring a shotgun. There's no better weapon in the dark," he said in a deep, hoarse whisper.

"Fine time to be thinking of it."

Again Cameron chuckled. He felt in the dark for clinkers to block the rails and prevent the bug drifting back down the tracks. They began walking the rest of the way up the slope together, between the rails. Hewitt felt the regularly spaced ties vanish from under his feet, as they walked into pure cinder ballast. Cameron put out a hand to stop him.

"Here's where they dumped the engine grates. You could see it from here, if you was up high in an engine. On foot, it's a little further," he said.

They walked on past the engine ashes and were on bare ties again. Cameron put out his hand and stopped Hewitt. He pointed toward the cluster of yellow lights with his other hand.

"There, what do you see yonder, Jeff?"

"A windmill." It was the only thing that could be seen, the angular top of the tower, and the locked fan and windvane, outlined dimly against the starlit sky. There was nothing strange in seeing a windmill anywhere in this kind of country, but since there was nothing else visible, this meant something to Red.

"Yes, sir, a windmill," came Red's whisper. "You can see it for close to a half mile in either direction from up in an engine. Reckon a man on horseback would see it sticking up from just about any direction from quite a fur piece off—especially if he was looking for it."

"Or some kind of signal on it," Hewitt whispered.

"Yes. Listen, Jeff—on some days, there's a piece of red cloth hanging from that windmill top. Some days, it's white. Some days, it ain't there at all. And some nights there's a red railroad lantern up there, some nights a plain one—and some nights none at all. Engineers have raised hell about a red light sticking up there like that. Scares the hell out of them, and if it's their first time over the line, they go to the emergency brakes."

Cameron peered through the dark into Hewitt's face, while Hewitt stared at the windmill. Hewitt went suddenly rigid all over. Red sensed it and turned to look, too.

There was another shape on top of the mill. It could not be recognized as a man, in this dim light, but it could not be anything else. And suddenly a red lantern twinkled up there against the sky, as the man yanked off the cloth that covered it. He descended the tower swiftly, leaving the lantern suspended from the windvane. Both of them could hear the clink of his boots on the iron ladder.

"I'll be damned!" Cameron blurted too loudly.

"Sh-h." Hewitt clamped his hand on Red's arm. "I've got a hunch, Red. Do you know if there was a white lantern there, the night the train was stolen and your engineer killed?"

"Yes, there was. Fireman swears it."

"Keep your voice down! White means it's safe to come in—red means stay away. I'd bet on it."

"The State Line Gang!"

"Damn it, Red, keep your voice down! They're in the neighborhood somewhere, or they wouldn't be signaling them. That red light means us. Stay away while you and I are on the job!"

"Well, I bet by God I find out!"

"Not this way. You fool, you're just begging to be killed!"

Hewitt tried to hold the big railroad detective back, but Red was cold, tired, hungry and very, very angry. Hewitt stopped trying. "Then go it alone," he said. "I'll bring a wagon out to pick up your body tomorrow."

Cameron stopped, a dozen feet away. Instinct made Hewitt drop to a squatting position and take out his gun. Every hair on his head seemed to want to stand on end. The ear heard things, the eye saw things, the nose smelled things, of which the brain was not aware. And one thing was sure—they were not alone here.

Somewhere, a fence creaked. Wire shrieked briefly through a rusty staple, as someone's weight went on it. Red turned quickly, alert at last, and began striding swiftly back toward Hewitt.

The whole night seemed to light up as a shotgun went off, both barrels of a 12-gauge, Hewitt was sure. Red was pinpointed in the glare. Before it winked out, before Hewitt's ears stopped ringing, Hewitt knew that Red had been hit.

He scuttled toward Red, still squatting, keeping a low profile, and heard Red moan and slowly settle to the ground between the rails. Hewitt found him on his knees, trying not to pitch forward on his face. "Christ, I'm killed, Jeff," the big man whimpered. "I'm just full of shot."

"Get your arm across me. We've got to beat them to the bug."

"Get the hell back to town! Nothing you can do for me."

"Shut up and try to help me."

Hewitt got Red's weight across his shoulders, with a little help from Red. He was fearful of his own strength, after his illness, but his body responded perfectly. He almost ran down the tracks under Cameron's weight.

Red was able to help himself a little, as Hewitt put him on his seat on the bug. The thought that made Hewitt's skin crawl again was that whoever had fired at Red would not be sitting idle in the dark. There was no time to fish out the clinkers that blocked the wheels. Hewitt pushed hard, and with a grating sound the wheels crushed them and took the steep grade.

Hewitt leaped aboard and caught the moving handlebars. On the other side of them, Cameron had slumped forward, and the movement of the handlebars almost threw him from his seat.

Behind them, someone shouted, "Handcar! They got a handcar."

And that surprised you, didn't it? Hewitt thought. Aloud, he said, "Hang on, Red. It's all downhill. Have you to a doctor in no time."

Cameron did not answer. The car raced down the grade, its iron wheels screaming thinly on the steel rails. A bug was not the most stable vehicle on the rails. Anything could dislodge the light outrigger wheel, and send the whole frail thing spinning through the air. Hewitt found the brake with his foot, and tested it, but he did not use it.

Hewitt had to stand up and lean across the jumping, creaking handlebars, to hold Red on his seat. They gained so much momentum that they coasted almost all the way into town. Before the car stopped, Hewitt clambered over the handlebars in the dark, straddled the wooden saddle behind Cameron, and held him erect with one hand while he pumped with the other.

There was no sign of life at the depot, nor had he expected any. But across the dirt road that paralleled the tracks was the Railroad Saloon. There were no horses tied in front of it tonight—not as cold as this night was—but Hewitt fired two shots in the air and brought two curious faces to the door.

"Somebody give me hand, and somebody go for the doctor and Sheriff Gavin. I've got a man here with a bad wound," Hewitt shouted at them.

It was worse than that, he knew. He had been pretty sure he was riding with a dead man all the way down the hill. The lantern that someone brought showed the whole side of Red's face shot away, and his overcoat soaked with a great, red spill of blood from holes in his throat.

The young doctor that Hewitt remembered from his delirium was more upset over Hewitt, however. His thick accent was like Albrecht Raue's, but no one could mistake his meaning.

"It is damn fools like you who need doctor. I say take it easy, rest, eat, get well, and this is how you listen. It deserves you to die, Hewitt, because you are one big goddam fool!"

"I'm all right, Doctor," said Hewitt.

But he was not. He had to let them help him across to the Railroad Saloon, where he was enjoying a hot milk punch when Art Gavin arrived. "I don't know what happened. Somebody took a shot at us in the dark. Red wanted to show me something, but he never got around to it," Hewitt said.

"Hell of a note," said Gavin. But he caught the mute warning in Hewitt's look that said, *Later, later.* . . . It was much later, almost midnight before Hewitt felt like climbing the hill to Mystic's house.

The woman was waiting up for him anxiously, with the skillet hot on the stove and bacon sliced. Hewitt put away bacon, fried potatoes and three fried eggs, and felt better. Mystic was a good cook, the kind who enjoyed watching a man enjoy the food she gave him. And she was curious over what had happened, too, and not satisfied with the curt, stark outline Hewitt gave her.

He finished eating and leaned back in his chair. He reached across the table to touch the back of her hand with his finger. "Mystic, I have to talk some things over with Art, and I'll appreciate it if you'll leave us alone here a few minutes," he said.

She blinked, surprised. "Don't you trust me?"

"I don't trust the people who shot Red Cameron, my dear. The less you know, the safer you are."

"Jeff, I don't let anyone else run my risks for me."

"This time you do."

"I'm not sure I can let you talk to me like that."

"If I came into your bank and tried to tell you how to keep

your books, you would be insulted. This is a murder case, young lady, and as a criminal investigator, you're an excellent cook and bank auditor."

She stood up, showing her dimples in a smile, and patted Gavin's arm. "Art, watch this scoundrel! He's not the simpleminded fool he looks. Young lady, indeed. Oh, what gross, vulgar insincerity!"

But she left them alone. Hewitt listened and heard her bedroom door close, up in the front of the house. He and Gavin leaned toward each other.

"You don't trust her," Gavin said.

"I don't trust anyone. Well, Art, I'll amend that. I've worked with a lot of peace officers, and I have never met one I trusted as quickly as I have you."

"Yeah, but what happened? What *really* happened out there when your friend got killed?"

Hewitt told him. Gavin's mean little face hardened until it could have been chiseled from stone, and his small eyes glittered. "Somebody there is in cahoots with the State Line Gang," he said softly, at the end.

"Yes, and you're not really surprised, are you?"

Gavin avoided a direct answer. "You think old Porter Lansing is in on it?"

"How do I know what to think? Who works out there?"

"My deputy's brother, Meade Hutton, is Porter's manager. Porter pays him a pretty good wage, and I hear he takes a piece of all the profits."

"What is Meade Hutton like?"

"I wish his brother had half as much brains."

"Honest?"

"I never had no reason to believe he ain't."

"What kind of setup does Lansing have there?"

"Small house with two bedrooms. Meade Hutton lives in one, and eats in the bunkhouse. Porter keeps a cook the year

round, and three or four hands most of the year. More in hay-
ing time."

"Good men?"

"They suit him, I reckon."

Meaning that Gavin did not think much of the men hired
to work on Porter Lansing's horse ranch. There could be
many reasons for that, however. These tough old-timers like
Lansing knew how to get more out of cheap help than many a
man could out of the best. That was how they became rich
men in the livestock game that broke so many.

"I take it that Hutton is not a married man."

"No." Gavin seemed to debate with himself a moment.
"But he'd like to be."

With a slight nod, Gavin indicated the unseen woman in
her bedroom in the front of the house. They two leaned
closer together, and Hewitt whispered, "How does she feel
about it?"

"Ask her."

"Maybe I will sometime, but what's your guess?"

"Why do you care, Mr. Hewitt?"

"She works in the bank. I'm sure she has more authority
than she acknowledges. I can't believe anything goes on there
that she doesn't know about. And by God, Sheriff, I find it
hard to believe that anything goes on in this town that you
don't know about, too!"

"Mr. Hewitt, I've knowed a dozen men that would've
fought a mad bull bare-handed for Mystic McDonald.
Meade Hutton is one of them. Couple of years after her husband ran off, her and Meade went around together a little. In
fact, I reckon he was the first man she went out with after
that. But it didn't last long. There's been a couple of men she
went to church with, things like that. Mostly, she seems like
she's give up on everything in the man line.

"I don't think Meade is much of a talker, but his brother

did tell me once that Meade owned up he was still real deep
in love with Mystic. He told Bayard that there never was no
quarrel, nothing like that. She just seen he was in love with
her, and she wasn't in love with him, and wasn't going to be.
So she gave him his quit-claim, all in good spirit on her part.
Meade still aches, I think."

"I can understand that," Hewitt said. "She's a superb
woman. If I were a marrying man, she's the kind of woman I
would want to marry."

"Only you're not."

"No. Does it show that much?"

"Pretty plain to me. Only hope Meade Hutton don't jump
to no wild conclusions."

"They would indeed be wild. Was Mystic deeply in love
with her husband?"

"At one time, mebbe. But he was a piss-ant, Mr. Hewitt.
He just wasn't much of a man."

"What are you doing about Meade Hutton?"

"He ain't even in town. Bayard wired him to come back by
the morning train. He'll be here."

"Are you sure where he is?"

Gavin nodded. "If you're thinking he skipped to let these
State Line murderers have a clear path, you're dead wrong."

"I suppose the station agent wired the division about Red's
death."

"Yes, several times. They been on his tail for more information all evening."

"We'll have Burlington operatives here in droves tomorrow, you know."

Gavin's face hardened. "So long as they keep their place,
they're welcome. I need sleep, and I reckon you do, too. One
other thing, Mr. Hewitt. Otto Groshardt stopped by my
house this evening. He's real upset that you ain't been to see
him."

"He can wait his turn."

They shook hands at the door. Hewitt could hear faint sounds that meant that Mystic was still awake in her room, but she said nothing even though she could not help but hear Gavin leave. Hewitt went to bed. Shortly he heard her come into the kitchen and wash up the dishes from the meal she had given him. He was still awake when he heard her pass his door to return to her room. Tired as he was, he did not sleep for some time.

CHAPTER SIX

Just before daylight, Hewitt got up, dressed, and walked down the hill. He ate in Junkins' Saloon, which did a good breakfast business. He heard a train stop as he ate, and shortly two men came in, carrying suitcases, and sat down at a nearby table. Hewitt hid a smile. They might as well have worn signs on their backs saying "Detective."

He finished breakfast, paid the bartender, and stopped at the table to introduce himself. The two were Barney Fels and Neal Evanson, and they were not cordial. On a hunch that Meade Hutton had arrived on the same train, he went down to the courthouse, to the sheriff's office.

Gavin was there with two men who looked so much alike that they had to be the Hutton brothers. They were dark-haired, dark-eyed men in their early thirties. Meade seemed to be the older, and by far the stronger character. Bayard was trying to take down his brother's statement with pencil and paper, and was so nervous he was dripping with sweat. Hewitt closed the door and listened a moment.

"I write a kind of shorthand that I can turn into longhand later, Sheriff. Maybe I could help with this," he said.

Bayard looked at Gavin, who nodded. Bayard threw down the pencil with a sigh of relief, and Hewitt sat down at the desk. Gavin said, "Might as well start over again, Meade. Mr. Hewitt needs to know, too."

Meade Hutton narrowed his eyes and studied Hewitt

briefly. "You're the man that was took up to Mrs. McDonald's when you was so sick."

"Yes, I am."

"You're well now. Where you living?"

"I'm still at Mrs. McDonald's house, and to jump ahead to your next question—yes, the thought did occur to me that it might be better for her reputation if I moved elsewhere. She made it clear that her reputation *and* character were such that I need not worry. I don't intend to discuss it further, Mr. Hutton."

Meade Hutton said nothing, but he looked away and his stony face was full of pain. In a moment, he collected his thoughts and began talking as Hewitt took notes. Meade was not an educated man—far from it—but Hewitt was sure he had a good mind. Certainly he wasted no time on irrelevant details.

He had gone down near the town of Sidney to look at three colts Porter Lansing had sold last spring. The buyer refused to pay for them, complaining that they had not turned out well. Meade and the man were still arguing when Meade got his brother's wire. At this point, Meade almost smiled.

"I told him all right, I'd send him a check and he could ship the colts home collect. He changed his mind mighty sudden. You got to expect this when you sell a man a horse on a note. He's going to try to beat you out of it when it comes time to collect. Wouldn't be a good horse trader if he didn't."

"Sheriff Gavin just wanted this for the record," Hewitt said. "I think what he's mostly interested in is what you think of the signal that has been shown from your windmill tower."

Meade said flatly, "It's news to me. Somebody is going to get skinned when I run this down. But I believe you when you say it happened, Mr. Hewitt. The kind of men I can afford, I've got to ride their tails every minute."

"How is that?"

"Porter won't pay good wages, and he don't need to. There's a kind of man that will work practically for nothing, just to be around good horses. Them, and drunks, and crips, and old busted-up grandpas, is what I usually get," said Meade.

"Lately, ever since last spring, I been able to hire some able-bodied men for a change. I never thought much of it. Just felt grateful, I reckon. But my hunch is that some of them has been part of the State Line Gang."

A frank enough statement that faced suspicion squarely, Hewitt thought, or a magnificent bluff. . . . "A few Texans, maybe?" he said.

"Yes, three I can think of."

"One with a limp, from a short leg?"

"No. One out there now. I don't know his last name. You usually don't, when a man will work for twelve and a half a month. Calls himself Jed, which I reckon is short for Jedidiah."

"Good man?"

"Hell of a good man! Turns out a lot of work, is a first-class horseman, don't complain about anything. I wish I could find two or three more like him."

"What happened the night the engineer was killed?"

"I been all over that with Art."

"Go over it again with Mr. Hewitt," Gavin murmured.

"Mr. Hewitt, you'd have to see the place to know what happened."

"How about right now?"

"Suits me. Art, can you find him a horse? I've only got one in town."

Hewitt was not surprised to learn that Gavin owned three very good horses, and he would not have been surprised to be told that they had been bred on Porter Lansing's ranch. They saddled up and met Meade Hutton at the livery barn, where he had stabled his own horse when he rode into School Hill to take the train south.

They did not speak on the brief, two-mile ride out to the ranch, taking a winding, well-graded wagon road that paralleled the railroad tracks. There was another east-west crossroad at the ranch, which had a hilltop setting as beautiful as any Hewitt had ever seen. The windmill was turning rapidly in a coldly biting wind. Fine horses tossed their heads lonesomely behind strong corral fences. They sat their horses in the middle of the wide yard, while Meade told his story.

The little house where Meade slept sat in a grove of softwood trees, some distance from the tracks. The windmill was on the very top of the slope, the corrals and barns and the bunkhouse beyond it. From here, Hewitt could catch only glimpses of the rails themselves, but he knew that a train would have been quite visible, particularly at night, with the headlight burning.

Meade had been writing some letters in his bedroom in the house, and did not know the engine was in sight and had stopped nearby, until the cook pounded on his window and told him. He slipped into a coat, put on a cap with earflaps, and stuffed his mittens in his coat pocket as he went out. He also buckled on his gun, and then took pains to keep his gun hand warm by holding it against his bare stomach, under his shirt.

Not that he suspected anything then, but the State Line Gang was in the back of everyone's mind, and no man in his right mind went out at night unarmed. "Sounds like they're fightin' over there, Meade," the cook said uneasily. "I heard somebody scream, like to curdle your goddam blood."

"I don't hear anything now," Meade said.

Just then there was the clank and hiss of the steam-powered grate-shakers, as the gang forced the fireman to dump his fire on the tracks. The engine moved ahead a rod or so, Meade estimated, and the clanking continued. It stopped, and he could hear voices.

"All you'll do is blow the goddam boiler up, if you open the cocks and draw the pressure too fast," a shrill voice said. It was the fireman, still trying to argue.

Then the roar of steam, as the blow-off cocks were opened and left open. Hewitt surmised that the fireman had opened his injector at the same time, to let water into the boiler. Otherwise, the boiler might well have exploded.

The roar of escaping steam kept them from hearing the approach of the three men, who had to stumble through the brush in the dark. It was the horses that alerted Meade that something was wrong. He headed for the bunkhouse, to warn the crew there to put out their lights and come out armed. The cook trotted along behind him.

He rounded the corner of a fence, and that was all he remembered. He came to with his ears ringing, his head throbbing painfully. He could hear some man shouting, "Hungry, hell! No time to eat. Ride!"

Three horses thundered past him in the dark, turned on the crossroad, and clattered over the tracks. As Meade stumbled to his feet, he heard the riders turn north.

"I supposed they'd blunder right on into town, and I hoped to God somebody would recognize Port's horses and head them. But Mr. Hewitt, those men knew the country as well as I do. I bet I could show you how they rode right around School Hill, but the main thing is, they did it, and a stranger couldn't," said Meade.

"What about your other men?"

"Two stayed in the bunkhouse, which is just what I'd do myself, and at twelve and a half a month, you're just a damn fool if you don't."

"How many men did you have then?"

"Three. The other one—*by the Almighty!*"

"I'll bet the third man was Jed," Hewitt said.

Meade nodded. "He got knocked in the head and come stumbling out after they was good and gone—or he said he did. He said he was still dizzy and sick to his stomach."

"What'll you bet he's gone now?"

"We'll damn soon find out."

"I ain't seen him since he et supper last night, Meade," the cook said. "He didn't show up for breakfast."

The other two hired hands told the same story. They had heard the shotgun blast that killed Red Cameron, and had wished that Meade Hutton was at home. Like the cook, they were just holding down jobs, and not anxious to mix into anybody's trouble, especially if it was the State Line Gang. They had not even heard that Cameron had been killed, and they did not want to talk about it.

A double-barreled gunshot in the night, a man missing—what business was it of theirs? Nevertheless, Hewitt thought it would be worthwhile to get their impressions down on paper while they were still fresh, and he wished that he had his portrait crayons with him. There was no white paper that Meade knew of on the place, but he did produce a bleached muslin pillow slip that Hewitt pinned to the kitchen table in the house.

A saucer full of charcoal, culled from the ashpile back of the house, substituted for his crayons. Meade stirred up the fire in the big stove in the house, and put on a pot of coffee. It was clear that the hired hands here were not often in the house, if at all. Hewitt waited for them to get over the strangeness, until the kitchen warmed up a little. Meanwhile, he talked smilingly of other pictures he had drawn, that had helped solve other cases.

"First, let's decide how old this fellow was. We don't want to waste time trying to hit it too close—just enough to give me an idea."

"Fifty," said the cook.

"I doubt that, and I worked with him. Kind of a runt, but he could do a hell of a lot of work when he had to, more than you'd expect in a man of fifty," said one of the ranch hands.

"Forty," said Hewitt, "but a good drinker who had aged fast, maybe?"

"More like it."

"What color was his hair?"

"Black, what there was of it, with a bald spot in back."

Hewitt saved his muslin for a final impression, and reached for an old newspaper. "Thin face, or plump? Same width top and bottom, or did he narrow down at the chin?"

"Thin face, but wide at the eyes. High cheekbones, but not like an Indian. Kind of narrowed in at the temples a little, if you get what I mean."

"Like this?" Hewitt drew a few lines on the newspaper.

"That's it! Kind of pop-eyed, too, and scraggly eyebrows. Nose kind of flat at the end, like somebody busted it for him."

The final picture was put together from a series of sketches on the newspaper. Hewitt rarely trusted these pictures drawn from the memories of others, but he felt that this one might be a little more accurate than most. What impressed him was Meade Hutton's admiration for it.

What emerged was a smallish man with a gaunt face, a taut mouth slightly twisted and slanted to the left, the broken nose of an old saloon fighter, a deeply furrowed forehead and lank, sparse black hair only slightly shot with gray. Growing thick over ears and temples, it merged with a month's growth of straight, black beard with more gray than the hair on the head.

It was a familiar type to Hewitt, although the man himself was unfamiliar. A born renegade, sly but not smart, mean but not nervy, one of mankind's culls who would never be anything but a cull. The Texas border country was full of them.

He rolled the muslin up carefully between sheets of newspaper, and returned to town with Sheriff Gavin. He bought a pint of clear varnish, thinned it liberally, and carefully brushed the entire sheet of muslin with it, to stiffen the muslin and "fix" the charcoal. He hung it in the window of the sheriff's office, with this legend in big, strong letters below it:

WANTED: THIS MAN!

Only known name is "Jed." Speaks with a Texas accent. Good horseman and hard worker. He is wanted for questioning in connection with a murder, and no doubt will be armed and dangerous. Do NOT try to question or arrest this man yourself!

A. E. Gavin, Sheriff.

He took time to go to the barber shop for a shave and haircut, before calling on Otto Groshardt. The American Eagle Bank was housed in a brand-new brick building with a brick floor. Its huge steel safe was not encased in the building itself, but stood out prominently near the front door. It was good business, and more and more country bankers were keeping the bank's money where the clients could at least see the safe where it was stored.

Groshardt did not sit behind a railing. His desk was also near the door, where he could personally greet everyone that came in. He knew Hewitt the moment he saw him, and his blue eyes narrowed in his big sea-chart of a face. He stood up and offered his hand, a powerful, bulky man of perhaps fifty.

"Mr. Hewitt, I believe. You took your time coming to see me, didn't you? I suppose you have your reasons, but they are not clear to me at this time," he said.

"I'm sorry if I neglected you, but I've been both sick and busy. I hope I'm still in time to help Albrecht Raue," Hewitt said, taking both Groshardt's hand, and the chair at the end of the desk that the banker invited him to take with a wave.

Groshardt waved the hand again as he sat down. "They cannot convict Albrecht. Perhaps it will be a good lesson to them if they try. I'm not so concerned about him. There are other things that worry me more."

Groshardt's accented English was better than Hewitt's. Hewitt remembered the man's story. The oldest of a big family of Prussian peasants, Otto had been sent to England when he was only fourteen, to learn the language and prepare for emigration to the United States. He had come over at age eighteen, worked two years as a schoolmaster, three more for a lawyer, reading law. There had been only a few German settlers in School Hill when he came here and opened a law office.

One by one, he brought his brothers and sisters over. Swiftly, the family accumulated land. It was hard to guess how much wealth the family controlled now, but it was at least a quarter of a million dollars, and probably closer to half a million.

"I think I differ with you about Raue. It doesn't do much good to a young man's reputation, if a jury isn't able to convict him because of the lack of conclusive evidence. All his life, people will wonder if he really killed that man. The only way out, Mr. Groshardt, is to convict the man who did do the job," said Hewitt.

"And who is that?"

"We keep coming back to the State Line Gang."

Groshardt turned an angry pink. Someone was coming toward his desk with a paper to be signed. He waved the man away, stood up, and gestured to Hewitt to follow him. They went to the back of the room and through a door into a room with three small, high, clerestory windows. It was furnished only with a big table, eight chairs, and a small secretarial desk. This, Hewitt knew, was where the board of directors of the bank met.

Groshardt closed the door behind them. "The State Line Gang, what nonsense!" he said furiously.

"I saw them. They're not nonsense," said Hewitt.

"You saw somebody. You seem to believe that there is an organized outlaw gang that moves back and forth from South Dakota to Nebraska, run by an outlaw leader, something like the old Jesse James gang."

"Something like that."

"Complete nonsense! That's what this old fool of a Lansing thinks, too. Stupid old cowboy, that's all he is. Infatuated with tales of the old Chisholm Trail, always talking of Sam Bass and Billy the Kid and—and—what's the name of that other one? Lansing owns his gun."

"Wes Hardin?"

"Yes. Porter Lansing is senile. He has no business running a bank." Groshardt was so angry he was sputtering. "Six bankers had a meeting about this so-called State Line Gang. Do you know what Port suggested? That we find someone like Wyatt Earp, and pay him five hundred dollars for every dead body! Mr. Hewitt, if you get enough gossip going about a thing like this, you can actually create something that did not exist before. Make people believe in it, and it will come into being."

"You're not teaching me anything new, but—"

"No buts! The State Line Gang is a creation of someone's imagination. It would not exist, if someone had not had this dream of times that are past."

"You're probably right, except that how sure are you that Porter Lansing created it? I have reasons of my own for doubting his judgment on such matters. But take my word for it, he is *not* the evil genius who created the State Line Gang."

"He will break his bank. Our bank will pick up the pieces and become wealthier—true, true. But many people will be ruined. The community will suffer."

"What you're really saying is—"

"Do not put words into my mouth, Mr. Hewitt. I will speak for myself, and what I say is that Porter Lansing is an old fool who will destroy a good part of School Hill in his romantic—"

"Goddam it, Groshardt, shut up and listen to me!"

Hewitt took the banker's arm in a firm grip, and refused to let go when Groshardt tried to pull loose. "Let go of me," Groshardt said, dropping his voice. "I give you five seconds to take your hands off me."

"Go to hell." Hewitt retained his grip and went on, savagely: "What you're really saying is that there is not room for two banks here."

"You may think what you please, but I—"

"Shut up and listen! If you and Lansing are going to squander so much time and money and energy on libeling each other, one bank is a cinch to go broke. The first thing I want to get into your thick head is that Bankers Bonding & Indemnity Company is not going to get caught in a squeeze like that."

"There are other bonding companies. We can—"

"Try getting another bond with the State Line Gang operating so freely this close to town. Try to get another bond, after other companies find out that we canceled you out."

"I have known Conrad Meuse for—"

"Let's both send him telegrams. I'll bet you a thousand dollars to a hundred of your money, right now, that you have a wire back within twelve hours, canceling your bond. I do the field investigating, not Conrad. I make those judgments, and Conrad knows I have never been wrong."

The banker controlled himself, not bothering to strike a pose to save his own dignity. "You have a gun in my back, of course, but I am not going to be bullied. I want to know one thing from you, Mr. Hewitt."

"What's that?"

"Why are you living in the home of that woman?"

"I was taken there when I was too sick to know what was happening. It exactly suits me, and I don't intend to listen to any gossip that will reflect on either Mrs. McDonald or myself."

"Mr. Hewitt, I didn't give a damn about your personal relations with Mystic McDonald. You may both go live in a cave, for all of me. But she is the brains in that bank. She can't help but know what is going on!"

"What do you say is going on?"

"If I knew, I wouldn't need you, would I?"

"Do you think she and Lansing are embezzling from the bank, is that what you mean?"

"I don't know what to think. I merely know that Porter Lansing is a mad old cowboy and Mystic McDonald is a lot deeper than she looks."

Groshardt seemed to make up his mind suddenly. He took Hewitt by the arm, saying, "Come with me. I want you to see something!" They returned to Groshardt's desk. He unlocked a bottom drawer, took out a small piece of ruled paper, and handed it to Hewitt. It appeared to be part of an old personal letter, on which someone had later made a separate notation. The handwritten line from the letter said:

. . . etland getting prity frisky, time to put on the hobels, well I reckon I know how to . . .

The letter had jumped to another page here. On the margin, someone had carefully printed:

CXYE YMIIXAE TCEXYI

"Where did you get this?" Hewitt asked.

"Boy brought it to me. No need to bring his name into it but he's a sort of relative of mine."

"Nephew?" Hewitt smiled as he said it.

"Someone who knew I might be interested in it."

"Why would he think that?"

"Mystic McDonald dropped it from her purse when she was buying groceries in the store, as she was on her way home from the bank. She—"

"When was this?"

"Near the end of last June. For several years, Porter Lansing raised Shetland ponies out there on his place, did you know that?"

"No. I have known a few men who made fortunes raising Shetlands, though."

"Porter didn't. Shetlands are a luxury for rich kids, and you've got to showcase them where rich kids can see and want them. He sold out the last of his a couple of years ago. Pretty plain to me, someone is reporting back on one of them. One of his illiterate, old-fogy friends."

"Possibly. May I have this?"

"Yes, of course. Want to know why I feel that may be important to you?"

"Let me guess. That's Porter Lansing's printing, the code part, isn't it?"

Groshardt looked rueful. Then he grinned. "Damn it, Hewitt, it's impossible to stay angry with you! You're a slicker, that's what you are."

CHAPTER SEVEN

The two railroad detectives, Barney Fels and Neal Evanson, were not brilliant men, nor tough like Red Cameron. But they were old hands at this game. They knew that any criminal investigation is mostly plodding drudgery, and they had already volunteered to help Sheriff Gavin out with that. They had visited the livery stable, the barber shop, both saloons. They had brought fifteen men to the sheriff's office to look at the sketch Hewitt had drawn of the missing Jed.

Hewitt talked to them in the depot. They had found three men who recognized him. Not one of the three could give him a name, but they were good witnesses. All three had seen Jed *in School Hill.* And they had seen him there last spring, *before* he went to work for Meade Hutton at Porter Lansing's ranch. They had turned their witnesses over to Gavin.

This, Hewitt thought, doesn't tell us anything that we didn't already surmise. . . . Gavin was about through with his questioning of the three when Hewitt came into the sheriff's office. Hewitt warmed himself at the stove and listened.

"I can't think of anything else. Can you, Mr. Hewitt?" Gavin said, at last.

"One thing occurs to me, if you haven't already covered it," said Hewitt. He looked at the three witnesses, all middle-aged workingmen. "When you saw this fellow, Jed—was he alone?"

"Was when I seen him," one spoke up. "Like I told Art, he was mounting up in front of Shorty McClain's store. Had a gunny sack full of canned goods and so forth. I can tell you about his horse, if that'll help."

"It may help a lot."

"Good brown gelding, some white on his face. Not what you'd call a beauty, but good chest and legs. Kind of a horse that will go and go and go for you. And a kind of a funny brand on him."

Hewitt picked up a piece of paper, took a pencil from his pocket, and drew a *rúbrica,* an elaborate Mexican brand consisting of a long, wavering line crossed or forked by shorter, straight lines.

"Like this?"

"Yes, quite a bit like that. What you'd call a Texas brand."

Hewitt looked at Gavin. "This Shorty McClain—who is he?"

"Runs a little grocery store. We can talk to him, see if he remembers this fella, and what he bought."

"Sounds as though he might be buying grub for more than one person."

"I admit that idee crossed my mind." Gavin nodded for Hewitt to go on.

"Was he alone when you fellows saw him?" Hewitt asked the other witnesses.

"No, him and another fella come into the livery barn several times," one said. "Don't remember that they put their horses up overnight. Just grain-fed them and rested them, seems to me like. Man with this fella was a sort of old man. White-haired, in fact."

The third witness spoke up. "Same man I seen him with. He—"

"Wait a minute. I want to take this down." Gavin handed

Hewitt a pad of paper, and Hewitt sat down and began taking notes. "Where did you see these two together?"

"Twice. First time, I was helping George Alcorn find his milk cow. These two was camped up on Frazier Creek. Didn't think anything about it then. Early spring, and lots of boys riding through, looking for work. They make camp any old where, when they can't come up with the rent for a hotel room."

"Frazier Creek," Gavin murmured, "is nigh fifteen miles to the south of here, Mr. Hewitt."

The witness went on: "Week or so later, I seen them both in Junkins' place."

"Drinking?"

"A little, and eating hearty, too. I know the white-haired one paid up with a ten-dollar gold piece, because it was brand-new, and Junkins mentioned it after they left."

"When they left, where did they go?"

"Well, they had their horses tied in front of the Dutchies' bank."

"The American Eagle?"

"Yes."

"Mounted up right away and rode off?"

"Well, no. They was there a while. One of 'em's horse was carrying a stone in the frog of his foot, and they took turns trying to dig it out. Finely they did."

"Can you describe this older fellow pretty well?"

"Mebbe. White-haired, but a mighty good man yet, if I's any judge. One of them, you see, that turned gray early. Good heft of a man, at least a hundred and ninety pounds. Goddamdest pair of shoulders on him you ever seen. Real thick neck. He had on this high-crowned hat, you see, like you can buy down in Texas, on the border. But he needed a haircut, and you could tell it was white."

"Let's try to sketch him, and you two help me out. Maybe we can come up with a likeness as good as the one we have of the missing Jed."

There was charcoal in the morning ashes from the stove, which had not been dumped yet. Gavin found a piece of flowered wallpaper that was white on the reverse side. Hewitt pinned it to the desk and sketched swiftly.

"Like this?"

"Hell no, more jaw than that. You'd have to hit him with a club to knock him out."

"How's this?"

"That's getting it."

"How did he wear his hat?"

Neither witness was entirely satisfied with the quick portrait, but Hewitt did not press to perfection. He shook hands with both men, thanked them warmly, and offered to buy them drinks and supper next time they met. They went out, leaving Gavin and Hewitt alone. The sheriff came over to stand beside Hewitt to study the sketch.

"Anything strike you about it, Sheriff?" Hewitt asked.

"No. He's a stranger to me."

"To me, too. But suppose you got only a quick glimpse of him, under an overcast sky, with sheet-lightning flashing. That white hair could easily be mistaken for blond, and he's built like a young man."

"By God, he looks like Albrecht Raue!"

"Not really," Hewitt said. "Same general build, and if you mistake white hair for blond, you assume a young man to go with it."

"Then Dick Lansing didn't really lie."

"I never thought he did, Mr. Gavin, but that's the hell of it with eyewitnesses. They can honestly say what they saw and still be wrong, because what they saw was wrong."

"What do we do now?"

"Why, we don't show this sketch to anyone, because it doesn't look enough like the man to be reliable. But we put out a good physical description of him. And if we want to surmise a little, I never knew a man with hair like that who wasn't called 'Whitey.' Here's your murderer of the stranger beside the bank—the man we have to hang to get Albrecht Raue out of a pickle. A man called Whitey, about sixty years old, six foot one, hundred and ninety pounds, vigorous and active as a man half his age. And he owns, or has owned, a twenty-two rifle."

"That's worth printing up and circulating—that, and a description of Jed. Mr. Hewitt, here's two members of the State Line Gang, and we didn't see either one of them the night they tried to lynch Albrecht, did we?"

"No, because it would have given away the whole organization. I guess you don't know this Whitey?"

"Never saw him around. Never saw Jed, either."

"So they were staying quietly out of the way of the law." Hewitt took out his wallet, and showed Gavin the slip of paper Otto Groshardt had given him. "Make anything of this, Sheriff?"

"Some kind of a code, this part."

"Yes. Recognize the printing?"

"Not well enough to get on the witness stand and swear it."

"But you're fairly sure in your own mind."

"Yes. Yes, I am."

"Wonder if it would be worthwhile to ask Porter Lansing if he ever met anyone answering to the description of our friend, Whitey."

"I would just as soon put that off a while, Mr. Hewitt. I have to live in this town."

"I understand. No sense in pulling your weapon until you're sure it's loaded."

"Yes. Mind telling me where you got that?"

"I can't tell you that. But I can tell you where it came from originally."

"Where's that?"

"Mystic McDonald lost it from her purse."

Gavin flinched as from a physical blow. "I see. Make anything of that code?"

"No, not enough of it. It gives me a few ideas, but they're pretty confusing ones."

Gavin brooded over the piece of paper. He had little formal education, and was a slow reader, but he was smarter than he liked people to believe. Without looking up from the paper, he muttered, "You know, Mr. Hewitt, this *de*ducing you detectives do can lead you up some blind canyons where there's neither tracks nor water."

"You just bet it can."

"You must figger this ties into the murder some way, and if it does, it ties into the State Line Gang."

"Not necessarily in a criminal way. But, Mr. Gavin, anyone who uses a code is hiding something, and we're blind as long as anything is hidden from us. This could be perfectly harmless and innocent, but at the same time, it could be a leaf over a track we need to see."

"Let's just suppose for a minute. Don't take me serious, Mr. Hewitt. Let's say that Porter Lansing has got something to hide. I don't hold that against him. Like the fellow who wouldn't put his money in no bank because he didn't trust any business where they pulled the blinds down and locked the door in the middle of the afternoon, get what I mean?"

"Yes. Secrets are a banker's business."

"You get my drift. But what bothers me is Mystic being in on it. She—she—well, I've got a secret or two myself. And I tell you that this town don't have no idee how much it owes Mystic McDonald!"

Now, Hewitt thought, we're getting somewhere. . . . But the sheriff continued to brood over the note, keeping his thoughts to himself. In a moment, he looked up.

"You know," he went on, "Porter tried raising Shetland ponies for a few years. What I kinda wish is that we knowed where he sold them when he sold out. This looks to me like somebody might be complaining about one."

He pointed to the line in the letter that said, . . . *etland getting prity frisky, time to put on the hobels, well I reckon I know how to . . .*

"I heard about those Shetlands," Hewitt said. "But while we're supposing, try 'Sweetland' instead of 'Shetland,' and see if it doesn't make sense, too."

Sheriff Gavin dropped the paper as though it had caught fire. "Jim Sweetland! Why, damn my soul! When did this piece of paper turn up?"

"About the end of last June."

"And Port claims he hasn't heard a word about Jim Sweetland since he left here."

Hewitt smiled. "That may be a legitimate banker's secret, Mr. Gavin. Let's forget this piece of paper until we decide it means something. What can we be doing that might be more productive?"

Gavin drummed on the table. "Like to get out a lot of dodgeroos on Jed and Whitey. Like to offer a little reward, too. But that means a battle with my county commissioners, and I'd probably lose it. They been impatient with me ever since this feller was killed."

"How much would the dodgeroos cost?"

"Oh—fifty dollars to print up and mail out to sheriffs around here and in South Dakota."

"How much reward do you think it might take to turn something up?"

Gavin grinned his mean little grin. "Most men would turn in their own grandmothers for a thousand dollars. This time of year, a man out of a job would do it for fifty."

"My company will pay for the printing and mailing, and will put up one hundred dollars for the reward, fifty on each man."

"Mr. Hewitt, you *say* you will, but I'm the man who has got to meet the bills when they come due. Would you mind putting that in writing?"

Hewitt took the wallet out of his shirt pocket, just over his .38 in its shoulder holster. He rarely let anyone know that he carried money here, but he liked and trusted Gavin. He opened it and took out two fifty-dollar bills, two twenties, and a ten.

"You put it in writing yourself," he said, laying the money on the desk. "My partner is as tightfisted as your commissioners. I'll need a receipt."

"While I get it from the treasurer's office, why don't you write up what we want printed?" Gavin replied.

It did not take long to prepare the dodger:

$100 REWARD!

$50 Reward for Each of These Men:
No. 1: Goes by name of Jed. Speaks with Texas accent. Good horseman, hard worker but keeps to self. About 45 yrs., 140 lbs., slight build, going bald but hair & beard dark shot with gray.
No. 2: Probably known as "Whitey." About 60 yrs., powerful build & looks & acts younger. Height 5′ 11″, 190 lbs. Hair almost white, and when last seen, it was worn long.
NOTE: These men wanted for questioning in connection

with TWO brutal murders. Do NOT try to arrest them yourself! Notify nearest law enforcement officer or the undersigned.

Arthur Gavin, Sheriff

School Hill, Nebraska

The two railroad detectives, Evanson and Fels, came in as Hewitt finished. Silently, he showed them the copy. He could almost feel the reduction in hostility in them as they read.

"Who's putting up the money for this, B.B. & I.?" said Fels.

Hewitt said, "Yes. It's not much, but maybe it's enough to worry them a little. If they see enough of these posters around, it'll make them nervous, whether it persuades anyone to turn them in or not."

Fels nodded somberly. "You bet your boots it will! And don't you bet that someone won't squeal on them, either. Maybe one of their own pardners. Somebody, say, that ain't doing as well in the outlaw business as he thought he would. Somebody cold and broke and hungry and scared, and all he needs is a little running money. I tell you, Hewitt, when you're on the dodge, and you see these things staring at you everywhere—that's when you begin taking a second look at your pardners, and wondering which one of them is going to squeal."

"I hope so, anyway."

"I don't hope so. I *know* so. I was on one of them damned things myself, some years back. Anybody thinks it's a dirty, tough, miserable life being a railroad detective, he ought to try running from the law."

Less than an hour later, a telegram came to Gavin, notifying him that a United States Post Office in southern South Dakota had been robbed this morning, and the postmaster beaten insensible. More than eighty dollars in cash had been taken. More important, two registered letters, each containing a negotiable "bearer" bond for one thousand dollars, had also been taken. A local bank had been returning them to Chicago for redemption.

"Eighty dollars ain't much running money, and if they sell them bonds, they'll get about ten cents on the dollar," Gavin said.

"Ain't any guarantee it's the same people," Evanson said. "They didn't send no description at all."

"Didn't need to. It's the State Line Gang."

"How big you figger this gang to be?" said Fels.

Gavin shrugged the question off to Hewitt, who said, "My guess is that it's as big as it has to be for any given job. There's some one man who can pull them in as he needs them. They're not doing so well now, but it seems to me they're all hellbent to work when there's a job to be done. This suggests to me that they've got some really big stick-up planned for the near future. That's what's holding them together. I wish we could lay hands on the leader. He may not be as smart as he thinks he is, but he's ornery and bitter, and nobody's fool."

"Got any candidates with a name?"

"No," said Hewitt.

"I have," Gavin said; and the three took one look at his scowl and did not ask for a name.

Hewitt was tired, and it irritated him. In a case that could explode at any moment, he needed to be at his best. There was nothing to do but rest; however, before returning to Mystic's house, he plodded to the depot and sent a wire to his partner.

He sent it by the cheaper night rates, knowing it would be in his partner's hands by daylight. The two tipped every telegrapher freely, and the practice had paid handsome dividends. His message said:

MOST URGENTLY NEED CREDENTIALS EXAMINE BOOKS
OUR COMPETITORS CLIENT HERE STOP HEAD OF FIRM
SHD BE WIRED SOONEST EXPECT ME STOP MAY SAVE
BIG SUM FOR JIBC SO WARN I WILL NOT ASSIST OTHER
INVESTIGATOR STOP WELFARE OUR CLIENT AT STAKE
BUT WHY SHD WE STAND TREAT QMK

And, he thought, let Jersey Interstate Bonding Corporation worry about this one! And Conrad, too, as far as that goes. . . . Hewitt had conducted several field investigations for J.I.B.C. The company always complained of the high fees—and Conrad would drive a hard bargain this time.

A horse was tied to a tree in front of Mystic's house when he arrived there. Hewitt approached warily, concerned for Mystic's safety. The horse was only so-so, the brand a strange one. As he hesitated, wondering how to proceed, the door opened and Mystic gave him an almost radiant smile.

"Dear me, why so cautious, Jeff?" she said. "There's a young man waiting to see you, one I've always been very fond of. I've got coffee waiting, and I've made some cinnamon buns."

It was Albrecht Raue, and he came straight to the point, even before Mystic left the room to bring coffee. "I tell you, Mr. Hewitt, I'm tired hiding out. Nobody tells me nothing, so I come find out what's go on. I told you, nobody fights mine fights for me," he said.

Hewitt shook hands with him. "Got a good place to hide out?"

"Yes, but—"

"Then go back to it, and be patient a bit longer. Mr. Gavin and I are pretty sure we know why they tried to lynch you,

Al. We have a good idea who committed that murder. It's someone who looks enough like you to make trouble for you—especially if you're dead. But we need a little more time."

"I can help. Anything but hide out!"

"Hiding out is the only way you can help."

Raue started to argue, but Mystic said, firmly, "Albrecht, don't argue. You're not that stupid. I despise an ingrate. You know that."

"Ingrate? I don't know that word."

"An ingrate is someone who doesn't appreciate help from a friend. An ingrate is what you'll be if you make things harder for Jeff and Art." She turned, still smiling, to Hewitt. "I help in the school, you know, teaching English to older, immigrant children. I thought Albrecht was one of my brightest students, but I'm not so sure now."

"I ain't bright. By God, you know what I wish? I wish I could ask Buford Hunt what to do. He's smarter than anybody, and he know what to do."

"You forget Buford Hunt. All he can do is get you into trouble."

Mystic let Albrecht argue, and she soon had him grinning good-naturedly, and agreeing to do as he was told. She sent him on his way, full of coffee, cinnamon rolls and contentment.

"Al's a good boy, but it's so easy for a young fellow to go wrong at his age," Mystic said, as she closed the door behind the youth.

"He'll be all right. Who is Buford Hunt? The name is familiar to me, somehow."

She laughed. "He's an old-timer in Topeka. Until a few years ago, he came up here every fall at round-up time, but he's getting pretty old for it now. He knew all the old outlaws.

Albrecht met him when he was about fifteen, and he still hero-worships him."

"I guess I don't know him."

"He's the man who sold Porter Lansing the gun he prizes so much—Wes Hardin's. Hunt knew Hardin, Sam Bass, even Quantrill. It belonged to Hardin's lady friend."

"Oh yes, I place him now. I just never ran into him."

He found an excuse to leave the house soon, and get the depot agent out of his house to send another telegram. This one went to Johnny Quillen, ace operative of the Santa Fe, and one of the few men Hewitt really thought of as friends. Their friendship was based as much on mutual avarice as on mutual respect. Johnny liked money as well as Hewitt did. The wire to Quillen said:

SEND SOONEST ALL YOU KNOW ABOUT BUFORD HUNT STOP
SUPPOSED TO BE SIDEKICK WES HARDIN AND SOLD HIS GUN
TO COLLECTOR I KNOW STOP THIS ONE FREE BUT NEXT ONE
COULD BE RICH REGARDS ETC

CHAPTER EIGHT

A weekend had crept up, unnoticed, on Hewitt. On Sunday morning, Mystic asked him to go to church with her. He welcomed the idea, not because he was particularly a religious man, but because it gave him a new perspective on any town in which he had a case.

He knew that there were three churches in School Hill—a Presbyterian one, attended mostly by people who banked with Porter Lansing's Farmers and Merchants Bank, a Lutheran one, just as closely allied with Otto Groshardt's American Eagle Bank, and a Roman Catholic one that seemed to have no particular banking orientation. He was not surprised to learn that Mystic was a Presbyterian.

"We'll stop and pick up a girl I think you'll like. She teaches the seventh and eighth grades here," Mystic said, as he helped her on with her coat. "She's from Rome, New York, and to her, this is the Wild West."

"I've been in Rome," Hewitt said, for lack of anything better to say.

"Oh? Then perhaps you know her family, the Durants. I believe they're quite well-to-do."

He did not know the Durants. Beth Durant was not a girl, but a mature woman of at least thirty-two, with a magnificent bosom of which she was rather complacently aware. Hazel eyes, light brown hair, perfect skin, and the taut nerves of a Thoroughbred racer going to the post. It was this wild and restless something just under the surface that warned Hewitt that here was a woman who had fled West after disappointment in a passionate love affair. She was probably on the lookout for another, and he wondered at Mystic's motives in bringing them together.

Beth Durant lived with a German couple, Jacob and Christine Zollner, newlyweds of about sixty. An enormous, black dog came roaring to the door at their knock. The woman who opened the door merely spoke to him sharply in German, and the dog stepped back out of the way.

"He minds me, but nobody else. It's a good dog to have around when my husband is away so much," Mrs. Zollner said.

Jacob Zollner spoke almost no English, but his German was a kind in which Hewitt could carry on a conversation. Zollner was a wiry man of about average size, obviously intelligent, and with a merry disposition. He had just shaved, and insisted on showing Hewitt some new razors he had just received. When Hewitt expressed admiration for them, Zollner insisted on giving him a pair of them.

"Leave them here, and pick them up when you bring Beth back from church. My husband is so happy you can talk German with him," the wife said, beaming.

Beth Durant came out of her bedroom then, and the three went on their way to church. Hewitt walked between the two women, both so attractive, each in her own way. Beth Durant rolled her eyes at him and said, "It's not very nice of me to say it, but did you notice the atmosphere in that house?"

"Only that they seem very happy," Hewitt replied.

"It's a mail-order marriage. Christine came over from Schleswig as a servant, when she was past fifty. Jacob has been a widower for fifteen years."

"Oh? What does he do for a living?"

"He owns a farm, but he's a woodcarver, too. If you're

around long enough, ask him to show you his shop. It's really beautiful work."

"They're lovely people," Mystic said.

Again, Beth rolled her eyes. "Well, yes, but the honeymoon atmosphere gets a little overpowering. I wonder what kind of letters they wrote in arranging their marriage."

Mystic plainly did not approve of this kind of talk. "They are fine people," she said firmly, "and I'm glad Christine has the dog. Where did she get him?"

"The dog was his, but he never could handle him. You saw how it minded her! Its name, by the way, is 'Howdy.' Christine says that if you call it by name, it won't bite. I rather doubt that, myself."

It was one of those clear, cold mornings that brought people out of their houses to church, and the church was packed. Beth Durant had a splendid soprano voice, Mystic a competent alto. Hewitt knew that his own baritone was nothing great, but he had a good ear and had belonged to the post glee club in his Army days. He enjoyed startling both women with the vigor with which he joined in the singing of the hymns, and he enjoyed just as much the looks of pleasure that their three voices brought from nearby worshipers.

An earnest young minister preached a sermon that was neither brilliant nor dull, and Hewitt stayed awake by playing with the idea of living here, of settling down, of being a part of a community of people instead of the eternal traveler. Sitting between two attractive women made the thought even more attractive.

In one of those moments of silence that come in every crowd, a soft, snapping noise penetrated Hewitt's mind disturbingly. He wondered if he had not heard it just a moment before, and what it was, and why it should upset him.

He put it out of his mind to join in the singing of "Old Hundred," used as a collection hymn. He noted that Beth

Durant gave a quarter, Mystic McDonald a dollar. He slipped a dollar into the plate himself, but it was wrapped around a five-dollar gold piece. He had no doubt but what he would be identified with the gold and did not mind.

It was over at last, but then he had to stand in the icy vestibule with the young preacher and shake hands with dozens of people. They all knew who he was, and why he was here. Eventually, they got away.

He had not taken close notice of the way they had come to church, but there was some trace of unease in him that made him attentive to his surroundings as they headed back to the Zollner house. They skirted the town on the rounded hilltops, where winter-naked softwood trees waited for spring, which had to come sometime.

He heard the clink of a shod horse. "Listen!" he said. "That sounds very close."

"It is close," Mystic said. "Somebody's crossing the creek yonder." She pointed.

"And his horse needs shoeing. Calks are just about gone. He's slipping on plates."

"Oh, listen! You can even hear his saddle, and the panting of the horse. How sound carries!" Beth exclaimed, looking suddenly very beautiful in her excitement.

For another moment or two, he could hear a horse grunting as it climbed a frozen slope—hear the grating clink of shoes that were not getting a grip. And he had a brief but vivid picture in his mind of a silent man who wished his horse could be more silent.

"Where would he be going, Mystic?" he said, in a low voice.

"North. There's a way to reach the wagon road to the border, a short cut," she replied.

They heard no more of the horseman, and walked on. Nearing the Zollner house, Hewitt again felt that stab of uneasy apprehension. It was not the first time in his life that he had had such a hunch, and he had learned long ago not to ignore these things.

"I wonder if you could tell Mr. Zollner that I'll have to come back some other day for my razors. I've got something I really should be doing," he said to Beth.

Mystic said, "You can't do much on a Sunday, can you?" But the other woman seemed glad for him to have an excuse to come back some other time. She gave Hewitt her hand in a firm, friendly shake, thanked Mystic for bringing him, and started up the path toward home.

"See, I told you she was a lovely girl," Mystic murmured.

Hewitt only half heard her. The strange sense of foreboding deepened. He looked around quickly. They were traversing a path on a barren hillside. Most of the town was in view, and everywhere, he could see people going home from church—from all the churches. He heard the squeal of iron tires on frozen ground, and saw, far below them, Porter Lansing driving a team on an open spring wagon. It was a wild team, and the old man handled it well.

A woman's shriek, wild and hoarse and completely out of control, startled them both. His eyes met Mystic's, and she said, "It's Beth. Oh, my God, what's wrong?"

Hewitt suddenly knew what was wrong, remembering that strange, soft, snapping noise he had heard while in church. That was what made a .22 so deadly. It was almost a silent gun, under the right circumstances.

"Go get Art Gavin," he said.

"I'll come with you—"

He gave her a push. Beth Durant ran out of breath and then suddenly began screaming again. Hewitt said, "Get the sheriff, damn it, woman!" And began running.

Beth was standing no more than a hundred feet from where she had left them, staring down at the Zollner house with her hands at her cheeks. She did not know when Hewitt came up to her. She went on screaming, a wordless, witless sound that seemed to be ripped out of her by some force outside her body.

He seized her by the arm, spun her around, and said, "Shut up. Shut up, do you hear me? Make yourself useful. Shut up, I said, and come help me!"

She shut up and stumbled after him. Christine Zollner lay on her face in the dry, frozen sod near the tidy little house. Seeing no sign of her husband, Hewitt knelt beside the woman and took her carefully in his arms to turn her over. Her face showed clearly that she had been hit hard and hurt badly, but she was still alive.

"Open the door, and then let me go in ahead of you," he snapped at Beth Durant. "We've got to get her warm again. Hurry!"

Beth ran to the door of the house, which stood slightly ajar. Hewitt took time to take the .45 out of the holster clipped to his belt, before picking Christine Zollner up in his arms. He had to shoulder Beth aside to get into the house.

That the house had been thoroughly looted was instantly clear. Drawers had been pulled out of dressers and cabinets, and turned upside down. The new razors were gone. The house was cold because the door had been left ajar, but fires were going in both the heating stove in the front room and the kitchen range.

"Where's her bed?" he demanded.

Beth, still moving like a sleepwalker, opened a door. "The quilts and blankets are gone. Put her on my bed," she said, and opened another door. Whoever had looted the house had gone away without the bedding in this room, although the bureau and chest of drawers had been emptied, and two suitcases dumped upside down over their contents in a corner.

He put Mrs. Zollner down on the bed. "Cover her warmly

and get her shoes off. I'll put a teakettle on to boil, and you'll have to find jugs or bottles or something that you can fill with warm water and put in bed with her."

"She needs the doctor," Beth mumbled.

"He'll be here soon, you can bet on it. What she needs now is to get warm, woman! Is there anything to drink in the house? As soon as she can swallow, give her a hot toddy of some kind."

"There's some sailor rum—Jacob has a little every evening."

Beth seemed to be coming out of the daze that had made her so clumsy. Hewitt ran into the living room again, stoked the stove with wood and opened the draft and damper to get the fire roaring again. In the kitchen, he did the same with the range. The teakettle, already full of warm water, was on the back of the stove. Hewitt moved it to the front lid and went out, closing the door behind him. The house would warm up quickly now, and if Beth could get her wits back and do the things the woman needed done for her, Mrs. Zollner would live.

He found Jacob Zollner's body almost at once. Zollner had been shot through the head with a .22 that had entered in the left temple and come out near the right ear. He had died instantly, falling on his side in a heap just behind the house. Despite the icy cold, there was still warmth in the body. Zollner had not been dead long. Say, thirty or forty minutes, just about right to pinpoint it at that snapping sound Hewitt had heard in church.

What puzzled him was the missing dog, Howdy. He was sure now that he had heard not just one, but *two* shots. The first, beyond doubt, had disposed of the dog. But where?

Hewitt stood up and looked around, and just then the big dog came staggering over the brow of the hill behind the house. It saw Hewitt and put its head down and began running toward him. Its head was a horror, one eye gone and the skull above and behind it deeply creased. But it was alive and both ready and able to kill.

He knew the dog would be useful in tracking down the killer. He retreated from it to the kitchen door. He stepped inside and jerked the door shut just in time. The slamming of the door brought a sharp cry of fear from Beth in the bedroom.

"The water's about to boil. Let's get going here, and get that woman warm," Hewitt said.

Beth came into the kitchen and took out two clean, empty, well-corked whiskey bottles from a storage cabinet. "She's waking up, but she's suffering so, poor thing!" she whispered.

"You'll have to take care of her. Where can I find a rope or hitch rein?"

"In the front closet, next to the front door."

He left her and ran through the house to find a neatly coiled half-inch rope in the front closet, under Jacob Zollner's coat. He made a quick noose in the end of it, with a knot that he judged would keep the noose from closing and choking the dog to death.

Howdy was recovering fast. He came around the corner of the house the moment Hewitt let himself out the door in front, and he came on the charge. Hewitt shifted the rope to his left hand and holstered his gun. He got his feet under him and let the dog make his jump at his throat, and gave him his forearm to worry.

The sleeve of Hewitt's heavy coat protected his arm, while he hooked a foot behind the dog's two hind legs and dumped him over backward. When the dog came up, Hewitt caught him on the end of the nose with his fist. By the time the dog's head cleared, Hewitt had the rope on him. He hauled it up short, and then forced the dog backward.

"Sit, Howdy. Sit down," he said sharply.

The dog, out of habit, obeyed. It was in pain, and was something horrible to see, with that one eye gone and a bloody scar across its head, but there was still a lot of life in the brute.

People came swarming in within the next few minutes. Dr. Schickel and Sheriff Art Gavin arrived together. The doctor made a swift examination of the woman, with only Beth Durant in the room. Hewitt could hear the doctor's voice, and Christine's weak and broken one, in German.

"What happened, Mr. Hewitt?" Gavin asked.

"Catch the fellow who did this, Mr. Gavin, and you've got the killer who shot the man behind the bank," Hewitt replied. "Same gun, and I'll bet the same reason for the crime."

"What's that?"

"Somebody hard up for running money, is all. He saw the man behind the bank had money, and he shot and made off with it. He came in here and shot Zollner and beat up on his wife, and grabbed everything he could sell or swap from the house."

"And we won't find anybody that saw him."

"No, but I heard him, and so did Mystic McDonald and Beth Durant, the teacher. I'll need a good, tough, surefooted, well-shod horse, Sheriff, and a saddle gun."

"Ha!" Gavin grunted. "For what? You're not a well man yet. I'll put Bayard on it. He can raise—"

"No, I'll take the dog and go after him alone. Believe me, it will be easier and faster and safer." He told Gavin about the sounds they had heard that morning, as a horse with worn-out shoes crossed the frozen creek and fought its way up the frozen slope beyond. "He's not going to make any kind of time with that horse. And I think that dog can run from scent. It's worth a try. Let your deputy follow, but not too close behind me."

Dr. Schickel came out and joined them. There was not

much he could tell them from what Christine Zollner had been able to testify, but it helped to confirm Hewitt's own appraisal of things. Christine had turned Howdy out to run free at his usual hour. The dog spent the nights in the woodshed, and most of his days on a long chain that allowed him to get into the woodshed for shelter. She fed him about noon every day, and about an hour before that hour, let him loose for exercise.

"She says he's a good dog, never chases livestock, never fights with other dogs, never bothers anybody. The first they knew anything was wrong, they heard a gunshot. A .22, she said. Jacob went out to see what had become of Howdy. He was afraid some kid might take a shot at him. A .22 is a kid's gun," the doctor said.

He went on: Jacob did not come back. Christine started to put her overcoat on to go look for him. She heard the door open behind her. She turned around, with the coat half on and half off, thinking it was her husband. She remembered a big, beefy face half covered with white whiskers and a big fist coming toward her.

The next thing she knew, she was on her hands and knees, trying to get to the front door, which was swinging open. She reached it and closed it. Not until then did she remember the gunshot, her missing husband, and the man who had beaten up on her in her own house. She got up and stumbled outside, trying to scream.

No sound would come. She could hear people talking as they went home from church. She started down the hill, tripped over something, and fell down. She knew nothing more until she regained consciousness in Beth Durant's bed in her own house.

Hewitt left it to the doctor and the sheriff to break the news to Christine that her husband was dead. Mystic McDonald had joined Beth Durant in the room with the woman. She slipped out, shortly after Schickel and Gavin went in. She was not a woman to cry easily, and she was in good command of herself now.

"Art says you're going to take the dog and try to track this fellow. Are you sure you're strong enough?" she said.

"I think so. Nobody is ever sure."

"I feel that you have the right idea, Jeff. I talked with Jacob about the dog. Howdy is a boar-hunting dog, a good tracker, and big enough to kill if he has to. I—I wish somehow that I could go with you."

He smiled. "But you know you can't."

"No. Christine said they had nearly forty dollars in cash in the house. It's gone. He took her wedding ring, and some razors and other things. Think of killing a man for so little!"

"It's not a little, to him. It's running money. It's life or death, and that's just the way I like it."

"Good luck."

She offered him her hand, and then, impulsively, stood on tiptoe to put her cheek against his. She insisted that he bring the dog back to her house, and feed it and stuff himself before setting out. Howdy behaved perfectly when Hewitt took his rope and started off at Mystic's side.

"This is very hard on Art Gavin, you know," the woman said. "He's a good man, but he's no longer young. He's taking this case very hard. It would be wonderful if you could catch whoever is doing all these killings."

Hewitt went into the house ahead of her when they reached Mystic's home. Nothing had been disturbed. He stirred up the fires while she changed into other clothing, and then while she fixed a dinner for him and packed a bag of food to take on the trail, he got ready to ride.

Art Gavin showed up while Hewitt was eating. He had brought a sleek, tough little half-Morgan mare for Hewitt to ride, with a Remington .30-30 carbine in a good boot on the saddle. He also brought two telegrams that had arrived just a few moments before. The first was from Conrad Meuse, Hewitt's partner, and it said:

IMPOSSIBLE SECURE AUTHORITY YOU DESIRE BUT WILL TRY STOP WHY NOT DO WHAT YOU ARE SUPPOSED TO DO AND THEN COME HOME

The other one was from Johnny Quillen, the Santa Fe's ace operative. It said:

BUFORD HUNT AGE NINETY CAN GET MORE ACTION OUT OF TWO FINGERS CHEAP WHISKEY THAN CUSTER DID OUT OF CRAZY HORSE STOP HAS SOLD PAT GARRETS GUN FIVE TIMES TO MY KNOWLEDGE STOP WHY NOT ASK WHITEY CASKIE ABOUT HIM QMK WHITEY DID TIME STILLWATER WITH HUNT STOP UNDERSTAND WHITEY·YOUR AREA AND GUARANTEE HE WILL FABRICATE WHAT DOESNT KNOW STOP BUT COUNT YOUR FINGERS AFTER HANDSHAKE WARMEST REGARDS

Hewitt handed the telegram to Gavin to read. "We have a name for Whitey now," he said. "Mean anything to you?"

"No. You know this Caskie?"

"No, but I'll bet he's the man I'm looking for and the one you're looking for on the murder behind the bank."

The sheriff said slowly, "Mr. Hewitt, I want to send Bayard Hutton with you. He ain't the greatest deputy in the world, but he's got nerve and he can shoot. What I really wish is that I was twenty years younger."

"If you were twenty years younger, you'd be long gone on this trail yourself, Sheriff. It's a one-man job. You know that."

"Then I'm going to have Bayard foller you."

"A good half-day behind me, and see that he keeps quiet. This fellow is going to have to peddle some of the stuff he stole out of the house, once he puts a few miles behind him. He'll have to stop and talk to people, go into towns, visit ranches and farm houses. It's not going to be a hot pursuit, and I don't want him spooked by somebody firing at game behind him a few miles."

Gavin nodded. "I'll tell Bayard that. But I don't want to lose track of you, Mr. Hewitt, and I'm glad you don't object to Bayard follering you."

Hewitt smiled. "What good would it do for me to object? It's your county."

"That," Gavin said, "is just why a man of mine has got to be close to the action. You ain't accountable to nobody, Mr. Hewitt, but I've got to ask these people to vote for me. That makes a difference."

They shook hands. "It does indeed," Hewitt said. "If we spring the trap on this fellow, it will be a county job. That's a promise."

CHAPTER NINE

The dog, Howdy, and the mare, Bess, did not like each other, at first. Both were well trained, however, and anxious to please. Soon, in the way of animals, they had achieved an understanding that relieved Hewitt of many a decision. He kept the dog on a short rope, never letting him get more than twelve or fifteen feet ahead. The mare quickly learned to follow the dog without guidance.

From the first, Hewitt had been fairly sure that he was on the track of the killer, although Howdy had been uncertain in his early tracking. He did not "line out" on a scent until they were miles from town, in unfamiliar country. Hewitt did not claim to be a tracker himself, or to know all there was to know about handling dogs. But it seemed to him that Howdy was more and more sure of the scent, perhaps because he was recovering from his wound. He lunged hard against the rope, and seemed to pick up the scent as much from leafless brush as from the ground.

The frozen ground yielded very few visual clues, but during that first afternoon, Hewitt saw several places where he was sure the horse they were following had been handicapped by the lack of toe cleats. The brown mare Hewitt was riding was smartly shod and surefooted as a goat. It was an advantage not to be sneezed at.

The man he was following kept out of sight as much as possible, staying well below the heights, and wearing his horse out in climbing in and out of canyons. Several times,

Hewitt got off to rest Bess, and take out the short telescope that he carried in his coat pocket. It was only a three-power lens, but it had a wide field and was another important advantage over the man he was pursuing.

Soon, Hewitt learned to know where the trail was going to lead him, so well acquainted had he become with the fugitive's mind. The man was pushing steadily northward, overworking his tired horse. The few times he took a local wagon road, he pushed the horse into a run, leaving the road before it took a blind turn in wooded country where he might have been surprised by someone coming from the other direction.

He saw signs where the fugitive had got off his horse to relieve himself, but nowhere did he see any indications that the man had eaten. He had clearly stuffed himself in the Zollner robbery, eating everything in sight as fast as he could. Perhaps he had been able to stuff a few things into his pocket, but there was no chance he was riding as well found as Hewitt.

It was almost dark when Hewitt heard the bawling of somebody's milk cow, and the shouts of young boys. He pulled Howdy off the scent and turned the mare toward the sounds. In less than a mile's ride, he came to a small ranch house where a couple with three small boys were trying to make a living on grassfed cattle. It was somewhat of a surprise to Hewitt to discover, talking with the man, that he had left Art Gavin's county behind.

The rancher, whose name was Harrison, was not hospitable. He had heard of the State Line Gang but had never worried about it. He had heard of the murder in School Hill, but was not concerned about it. He was not impressed by a private detective, until Hewitt described the murder of Jacob Zollner that morning.

"He was only minding his own business, the same as you. But he's just as dead as if he had been hot on the trail behind the sheriff. Maybe you can take care of yourself, but can you protect your wife and kids from a potshot artist hiding behind a tree?" Hewitt asked.

"What is it you want?" Harrison countered.

"I want to put my horse up under a roof tonight with a bait of oats. I want a few hours' sleep in a warm room, knowing somebody will be standing sentry-go. I'll take the guard duty from midnight to daylight. If nothing happens by then, we can figure our man isn't going to bust in on us."

Harrison thought it over. "I got a neighbor few miles to the northeast, a widow-woman with young kids. Maybe I ort to bring them over, too."

"Good idea. But be quick about it! Don't get caught out after dark if you can help it."

Hewitt did the milking and feeding for the man, while Harrison went for his neighbors in a farm wagon. They did not get back until long after dark. By then, the rancher had stopped being unco-operative. It was a lonely life in these hills, and once the sun went down, it was easy to believe that every dark pocket in the hills held an armed fugitive running from a murder prosecution.

Hewitt ate fried eggs and fried potatoes for supper, and then slept on the floor behind a cast-iron heating stove until exactly twelve-thirty. He had long ago trained himself to wake up when he wanted to. He slipped on his boots and coat, and went outside. Harrison had been standing guard in the barn. He heard Hewitt open the door and came silently to meet him near the house. He was distinctly uneasy.

"Your dog has been having himself a fit the last couple of hours. Don't make no noise, but he'd sure like to git loose. Kind of worries me," he whispered.

Hewitt held onto Harrison's arm and let him lead the way through the darkness. It was a ramshackle little barn, but there were six horses and several cows in it, and the heat given off by their bodies made it warmer by far than the frigid outside. The dog whined shrilly but softly in its throat, as it recognized Hewitt. Hewitt dropped down on his knee beside the dog, wishing he dared strike a light.

Howdy was trembling all over his big, muscular body, straining against the rope that kept him snubbed close to a hay manger. Hewitt slapped his ribs reassuringly, and stood up. "I've got a hunch our man is prowling around somewhere close by. It suits me if he is," he whispered. "Let him stay cold and hungry, and I'll be right on his tail when daylight comes. Why don't you go in and sleep?"

"I'll go in," Harrison replied, "but I won't sleep. And don't you come around the house before daylight, Mr. Hewitt, because I'm going to drop anybody that does."

Hewitt remained in the barn with the dog, all the rest of the night. He was even able to stretch out on the ground next to the dog, and catch two more hours of sleep. When he woke up, Howdy was asleep beside him and was no longer tensely on guard.

Daylight came, and Hewitt and Harrison patrolled the place together. Less than a hundred yards from the house and barn, they came to fresh horse droppings. They were frozen hard, but they had not been there last night.

"He came this close, but he knew better than to come any closer. He probably followed you home with the wagon, with your neighbors last night. He'd have been in here long ago, if he hadn't known you were laying for him," Hewitt said.

"How would he know that?"

"Why else would you bring your neighbor here? Or maybe he saw my horse, or the dog. This is like hunting a wild animal, Mr. Harrison. A wolf or a panther will take chances only when it has to, when it's cornered. The rest of the time, it stays out of range. A fugitive from the law is the same kind of predatory animal with the same set of defensive instincts."

Harrison said thoughtfully, "You know, there's some mink dens on my land a few miles north of here. Somebody has trapped two or three mink there this winter. Whoever is doing it would be perfectly welcome to do it, if he only asked permission. I wonder if it could be this same feller?"

"I don't know. What's a good mink worth now?"

"Prime dark mink is worth six or seven dollars, but they're too smart for me. I never been able to trap one. Don't seem reasonable it's this feller, though."

"Why not? We know that he knows this country, your place in particular. We know he's desperate enough to kill for a few dollars. I think I would like to look at this mink run of yours, before I leave here."

He set out after breakfast on foot, carrying the .30-30 carbine and leaving the dog behind. The overcast seemed not so heavy this morning, with a chance that the sun would break through. It was as cold as ever, however, a brittle, numbing, dry cold that made the light breeze as penetrating as a stiletto.

Harrison's description of where the mink dens lay was a good one. Hewitt soon came to the little, frozen creek that emptied into another one, also frozen. The mink had their dens up at the headwaters of the little creek, where there was a year-round spring. Hewitt left the creek bed and circled widely to his right. He moved slowly, keeping to the shelter of the naked softwood trees, taking his time.

An hour later, he heard, distantly, the restless nickering of a hungry horse, and his heart beat a little faster. He dropped to his knees and began crawling the rest of the way. It was slow going, and he wished that he had had more experience in this kind of warfare. One good thing—down on his hands and knees, he was out of the wind, and felt warmer all over.

A few stunted lodgepole pines appeared, and dry, bristling gooseberry bushes and buckbrush. Hewitt judged that he had now circled above the spring that fed the creek. Again he heard the horse, and this time it was peevishly pawing the frozen ground with a shod forefoot. Hewitt crawled on, now hunching along on his left side, carrying the carbine in his right hand.

He inched his way up a little ridge, heard the merry tinkle of running water, and carefully thrust his head forward between the screening gooseberry bushes.

And there he sat, scarcely a hundred yards away, with his back to Hewitt. He had the .22 rifle across a rock, and was waiting with all the patience that he needed for his one shot of the day.

A big man, bigger than Albrecht Raue. Old black felt hat that had seen better days. Old knitted maroon scarf around the neck, and a denim jacket with an extra shirt under it. No gloves on the enormous hands.

Slowly, barely breathing because the fellow's senses would be as acute as a timber wolf's, Hewitt got out his little telescope. He put the .30-30 down to focus the instrument.

The man's face was turned the other way, but he could examine the gun closely. A heavy gun, for a .22, no doubt bench-made—a target gun, the only one of its kind. Long barrel, heavy breech and heavy, single-shot action.

The little gun spat viciously. The man did not tense as he got his shot, but he leaped up as though on a tightly coiled spring after he made it. He leaned the gun against a rock, and Hewitt could focus the glass on his face in a moment of triumph.

Amazing, how much he looked like the drawing Hewitt had made of him! Heavy, brutal face with small, deep-set eyes and a small, straight, tight mouth. Jaw like the share of a railroad snowplow. Not young by any means, but not as old as his white hair would indicate, either.

Hewitt put the telescope back into his pocket as the white-haired man ran to pick up his dead mink. Hewitt knew just enough about mink to know that it took an artist with a gun to hit one. He's a better shot than I am, and lucky besides, Hewitt thought. I have got to hit him with a ton of brick to impress him. . . .

The man sat down, took out his pocket knife, and began to skin out his mink before it could freeze. Under his denim jacket, high up on his belly, he wore a .45. The .22 would be more accurate than Hewitt's short-barreled saddle gun at this distance. Hewitt lay there in the cold and watched the man slit the mink expertly around each foot and then across the span of the hind legs. He put the knife down to use both hands to "case" the hide, by pulling the mink out of its skin endwise.

Hewitt slowly, silently, brought up the Remington .30-30. He pulled the hammer back to full cock, almost without a sound. He centered on the stock of the .22, just behind the action. A true hit here would disable the gun as a target rifle, for the time being, but without damaging the gun permanently.

He squeezed off his shot and saw the stock explode in splinters, and knew that he was having luck today, too. The big man leaped up with the half-skinned mink in his hand, and Hewitt called sharply, "Hold it! You get the next one right in the forehead."

He levered a new cartridge into the chamber of the Remington, without rising from a prone position. He could see the white-haired man searching for him, and knew when those deep-set eyes located him. The man kept his hands elevated.

"You got the drop on me," he said, "but I ain't got nothing worth taking, less it's this mink."

Hewitt said, "Can that, Whitey. Don't waste my time. Keep your right hand up, but bring the left down and unbutton your jacket. That's it, that's just fine! Now reach in there and unbuckle your gun belt and let it fall. Now, step right over the gun and walk toward me. Just like that, just like that."

Again, a tied horse complained hungrily not far away. Whitey stepped over his gun and paced slowly forward, his beady eyes never leaving the spot where Hewitt lay hidden. He kept walking, holding the half-skinned mink in his right hand, until Hewitt told him to stop. When Hewitt stood up, they were less than a dozen feet apart.

"Hell of a note, one poor man against another one," Whitey grumbled. "I told you, mister, all I got in the world is this dad-blamed mink."

"You don't know me, do you, Whitey?"

"No, I don't, and where'd you get that name for me?"

"Give me one you like better, then. Caskie—is that the rest of it?" A slaty coldness flicked across the deep-set eyes. Hewitt went on: "I was on the train you tried to stick up, you poor damned fool. I'm Hewitt, the detective. Mean anything to you? If it doesn't, let me warn you of one thing. Force me to kill you, and you'll be the ninth man I've killed. Now, let's go get your horse."

He could tell when Whitey gave up, and he knew, too, how far the surrender went. Whitey knew it was no use trying to talk himself out of this one. But he would have to be watched like a chained wolf, because he would risk almost any odds to avoid going back to hang.

Hewitt marched the man ahead of him to where the horse had been double-tied, by both bridle reins and halter rope, to an overhead limb. It was a badly gaunted, hard-ridden horse, but a good one with no visible brand. Behind the saddle was a blanket roll, pink in color, but dirty now, and lumpy with the loot from the Zollner house. Beth Durant, as well as Christine Zollner, could identify that bedding.

"Just hang the bridle over the saddle horn, tie the halter rope up so he won't step on it, and turn him loose. He won't get far away, and neither will you," Hewitt said.

The moment the horse was released, it headed toward Harrison's ranch at a fast trot. It soon was out of sight. Hewitt had Whitey raise his hands again. He leaned the .30-30 against the tree and took out his .45 to hold in his hand, while he searched Whitey for another weapon.

He found nothing. He walked Whitey back to where he had shot the mink. He let Whitey pick up the mink and the .22 rifle with the shattered stock. Hewitt picked up the .45 he had made Whitey drop.

"Let's go. Take your time, man, and don't try to get too far ahead of me. Or too close, either."

Whitey did not bother to ask where to go. The time for that kind of pretending was long past. He plodded along wearily, a broken giant who might be feeling his age for the first time.

Three men came riding to meet them, as the ranch came into view. "Hold it!" Hewitt said softly. Whitey came to a stop. Hewitt held up his left hand and called, "Stay out of my line of fire. I've got a prisoner, can't you see that much?"

It was Deputy Sheriff Bayard Hutton, with his two-man posse. One was his brother, Meade, manager of Porter Lansing's ranch. The other was Howard Junkins, who ran the saloon. Meade Hutton and Junkins reined in, but the deputy thumped his tired horse in the ribs and came straight on.

Hewitt saw Whitey Caskie look back quickly and then step to the left, to keep himself in the line of fire between Hewitt and Hutton. Hewitt dropped a shot between his feet with the .45 and shouted again, "Hutton, you damned fool, I've got a prisoner here!"

"Oh, sorry!" Hutton reined his horse out of the way. Hewitt saw Whitey give up and relax. Hutton pulled up beside the prisoner, but hardly glanced at him. "Art Gavin is sick," he said importantly. "I'm acting sheriff. Not just a deputy now, Mr. Hewitt. Board made me acting sheriff, so I'll be in charge from now on."

"Fine with me. Just stay out of my line of fire when I'm holding a prisoner. This is the man who killed Jacob Zollner. This is the man who committed the murder behind the bank—the one Albrecht Raue was wanted for."

"Good, good. I'll take charge of him. You don't have no authority to take prisoners, Mr. Hewitt. Me and my boys will take this fella in now, and thank you very much for your help."

Oh my, I'm surely going to have trouble with this fool, Hewitt thought. . . . He said, "Mr. Hutton, the man is my prisoner until I turn him over to you, and you'll damn well stand back until I do that. Start walking, Whitey—and if there are any shots fired, you'll get the first one in the back of your head."

CHAPTER TEN

By the look on Meade Hutton's face, he was torn two ways, ashamed of his brother's idiotic behavior, but too fanatically infatuated with Mystic McDonald to let himself like the man who was living in her house now. Junkins might go either way, in a clash between Hewitt and Bayard Hutton. As a home-towner, he would be on the acting sheriff's side, but he was not a fool, and would not easily be dragged into senseless folly.

Whitey began walking toward the Harrison ranch. Hewitt kept a half-dozen paces behind him, shifting the .45 from hand to hand before either hand could get too cold to be useless. Harrison came to meet them, and did not need to be warned to stay out of the line of fire.

"Ever see this fellow before?" Hewitt asked him.

Harrison shook his head. "Seen the horse, though."

"Where?"

"Over toward the railroad, few weeks ago. Not this man on him, though."

"What did the rider look like?"

"Why . . . middle-aged man, I'd say, with a full suit of black whiskers. Wore spectacles and a long black coat."

"Did you speak to him?"

Harrison shook his head. "I just didn't like the looks of him, so I didn't let him see me."

"Which could have been the smartest thing you ever did,

Mr. Harrison. I wonder if you've got a piece of chain on the place, and a padlock?"

"I got the chain, but no padlock."

"Some wire-cutting pliers, then? And some wire. This man is a double murderer. I'm turning him over to Acting Sheriff Bayard Hutton, but not until I've got him secured the way I want him."

Hutton sputtered, "I'll secure him. Good God, Mr. Hewitt, I told you, he's my prisoner. You have no authority to make arrests!"

"Better check your law on that, Mr. Hutton. I have made a citizen's arrest, which is all you can do here. You're in another county, and your writ doesn't run here."

"But by God, Mr. Hewitt, I told you, I'm acting sheriff by order of—"

"You're acting like a damned fool. Stay out of my way." Without taking his eyes off Whitey, Hewitt appealed over Bayard's head to the other two possemen. "First, let's get this man chained up. You know what he did to poor old Jacob Zollner. You can have him, but not until he's chained, so he can't kill anyone else."

Meade Hutton looked at his brother. "Come on, Bay. It's just common sense," he growled.

"I'll do it myself. I'm responsible for the prisoner. I'll secure him myself," Bayard said.

"Just so it's done," said Hewitt. "Mr. Harrison, can you let us borrow your chain and pliers, and find us a length of wire?"

Last night, Harrison had been all hostility and suspicion toward Hewitt—now, he was on Hewitt's side and against the three possemen. He offered the chain, pliers and wire to Hewitt first. Hewitt shook his head, and Harrison handed them to Acting Sheriff Bayard Hutton, who slid off his horse and approached the prisoner.

"Pull up your right sleeve," he ordered. "One wrist and one ankle will be enough, if you behave. It's up to you."

"Watch him!" Hewitt warned.

It was as though he was seeing something that had already happened, in his memory, so sure he was of what both Hutton and Whitey Caskie were going to do. Hutton holstered his gun carefully, and carefully buttoned his coat over it so the prisoner could not get at it. He snipped off a ten-inch piece of heavy, galvanized wire, ran it through the end link of the chain, and held it out toward the prisoner.

"Let's have your wrist," Hutton said.

Whitey extended his right hand, his left one holding the coat sleeve back to expose his powerful wrist. Hutton pulled the end of the chain around it and probed with the wire for another link. Hewitt moved swiftly sidewise, as he saw Hutton come between him and the prisoner.

Whitey moved too fast. His big hand clawed at the chain. He wrapped it around his fist and drove the fist into Hutton's face. He caught Hutton before he could fall, swung his body up to cover his own, and felt for Hutton's gun under his coat. He dropped the chain as he found it and got his grip.

"Nobody moves, nobody moves, or this is one dead son of a bitch. You!" Whitey said, looking at Meade Hutton. "You're his brother, ain't you?"

Meade had to gulp twice. "Yes."

"You want to take him home alive, get off that horse and lead him to me. And you know how to do it if you want your brother back."

Meade looked helplessly at Hewitt. Hewitt said, "Do as he says. It's all we can do. He's got the drop." He let his own hands show, palms outward.

Meade dismounted and led the horse toward Whitey. Whitey let him come to where he could thrust the muzzle of the .45 into Meade's stomach. Then he let Bayard Hutton collapse on the ground.

"Let's have your gun," he said.

"Help yourself," said Meade, raising his hands.

Whitey lifted Meade's .45 out of the holster under his coat, and thrust it into his own belt with his left hand. It was almost possible for Hewitt to admire him, he was so cool. I have been in worse scrapes than this, Whitey seemed to be telling himself, and I have got out of them, too. . . .

"Set down over there," Whitey said to Meade, pushing him with the gun. "Turn your back to me and just set down. Now you come here, detective, and let's have your gun, too."

"Sure," Hewitt said. "You're not going to have any trouble with me. You've got the drop."

He kept his hands up and walked toward Whitey, until he, too, was close enough for Whitey to push the muzzle of his gun into Hewitt's belly.

"Unbutton your coat, detective. Slow, now—slow!"

"Sure!"

Hewitt unbuttoned his coat. His .45 lay exposed in the holster he had designed himself. It was tucked under the belt that held his pants, almost horizontally, apparently ready to fall out if Hewitt but leaned forward. Whitey dropped his left hand on the gun, which was held by a pawl that trapped the front sight in the holster.

"Take it easy! Just twist it, and it will come right out," Hewitt said. "Don't get nervous, now, and shoot me. Just give it a twist."

Whitey gave it a twist. The gun came free, and Hewitt lunged against him and got his foot behind Whitey's leg. He ignored both guns and butted his head against Whitey's big jaw as they went down together, Hewitt on top. By the way Whitey fell, Hewitt knew he was at least stunned a little.

He snatched the shot-filled leather sap out of his hip

pocket and swung it once, just as Whitey raised the gun in his right hand and fired blindly into the air. He caught Whitey in the middle of the forehead with the sap. Whitey went limp. Hewitt kicked both guns aside as he stood up. He picked up his own gun and then took the one from Whitey's belt that had belonged to Bayard Hutton.

Harrison and Junkins were still too startled to have moved, but Meade Hutton was up on his feet like a panther. Hewitt said to him, "The chain, quick, and the pliers! Let's get him secured before he wakes up—and this time, I'll do the chaining."

He was not sure Whitey was alive, and he took no chances. He wired one end of the chain around the man's huge wrist. He pulled the chain between Whitey's legs, wrapped it once around his body, and then pulled it back between his legs again. He wired the remaining short end to Whitey's other wrist, just as Whitey began moaning softly to wake up.

"Jesus God, he's dead! There's no heartbeat, Mr. Hewitt," Meade Hutton said, kneeling beside his brother's body.

"I'm not surprised. This fellow could break your skull with his bare hands, and he had a chain wrapped around his fist this time," Hewitt said.

Meade stood up slowly. There was murder in his eyes as he looked at Hewitt. "Lord, lord," he said. "How am I going to tell his wife?"

"That you did the best you could. That we all did. Help me get this animal on his feet, Mr. Hutton. We've got to get him back to School Hill in shape to stand trial for two murders."

Whitey stopped moaning as he became conscious. Hewitt prodded him with his toe and said, "On your feet, Whitey." Whitey felt the chain pull tight as he rolled over on his face. He grunted once, a choking sound of fury and defeat, and managed to get to his feet. His eyes were blank from the blow with the sap, and he was not sure what had happened.

"Mr. Harrison, I think we ought to have a bait of grub, and then we would like to rent a team and wagon to get our prisoner and our dead back to School Hill," Hewitt said.

"There's a faster way. You'll never get to School Hill until way after dark by road. I can get you to the railroad in time to flag a train, if you can do without eating. You'll be in School Hill by four o'clock."

Before parting with Harrison at the railroad, Hewitt wrote a note to Conrad Meuse: *Please forward $50 to F. A. Harrison, Berne Junction, Nebr., upon receipt of this. J. Hewitt.* On the back of the note, he wrote the address of Bankers Bond & Indemnity Company of Cheyenne.

"You'll have to wait for your money, because I don't carry enough to pay my bills everywhere. But I can advance this much in cash," Hewitt said. He slipped a pair of twenty-dollar gold pieces into Harrison's hands, along with the note.

Harrison shook his head. "I don't need to be paid for this, Mr. Hewitt. We all got to do our share."

"Correct, and my advice would be to get yourself a 12-gauge shotgun and some shells loaded with BB or buck. I hope I'm wrong, but you still could hear from the rest of the State Line Gang," Hewitt said.

The chained prisoner muttered, "The State Line Gang. There ain't no such thing. That's just a lot of talk."

It was the first word he had spoken since his capture. All the way from Harrison's place, he had sat in the back of the wagon, his feet dangling out. Behind him sat Hewitt, with the big dog tightly controlled under his left arm. It had not been necessary to warn Whitey Caskie that the dog knew him and remembered yesterday at Jacob Zollner's house. The last thing in the world that the fugitive wanted was to be on foot, both hands chained, with that big dog after him.

The train was pounding around a distant curve to the north. Meade Hutton and Howard Junkins stationed themselves on the tracks to wave their hands and flag it down. Hewitt offered Harrison his hand. The rancher took it with a somewhat puzzled look.

"What's he mean, they ain't no such thing as a State Line Gang?" Harrison said.

"He's right, in his way. Idiots like him start these gangs. People like us name them and wipe them out. Just when they're becoming well known, suddenly they're out of business," said Hewitt.

Whitey's big shoulders slumped. Harrison muttered something about how sorry he was he had not been more friendly last night. "I'll come back and see you some summer. Your wife can fry some chickens and boil up some corn, and we'll start over again," Hewitt said.

On the train, Hewitt sat beside the chained prisoner in the forwardmost seat in the day coach. Just behind him sat Meade Hutton and Howard Junkins. Only once did the prisoner speak.

"You sure went to a lot of trouble to make friends with that goddam ignorant farmer, detective," he said.

Hewitt chuckled. "Yes, I did, didn't I? Well, Whitey, my business is something like yours. We never know when we're going to need a friend, do we? The difference is, I have them when I need them, and you don't."

Hewitt was at supper in Sheriff Gavin's house when Meade Hutton came to report that Dick Lansing had viewed the prisoner. Without prompting of any kind, he had exclaimed, "Well my God, that's the man I saw in the alley beside the bank. Not that Raue kid—this fellow!"

"That's good, Meade. You keep the office open tonight for me and watch that man! Tomorrow, I'll talk to the county commissioners and Porter Lansing, and we'll see about things then," Gavin said.

"I ain't sure I want the job," Meade growled.

"Why not?"

"Don't think I'd make a very good lawman."

It was Hewitt's turn to ask, "Why not?"

"I can't take things in my stride the way you and Art does. I like to died, breaking the news to Bayard's wife. And even if that son of a bitch did kill Bayard, I don't want to see him hang."

"Not even for Zollner's death?"

Meade thought it over. "Well, that's different. That was cold-blooded murder from ambush. But Bayard got himself into it. Seems to me a man's got a right to try to break loose if he can. If he can't, tough luck. But if a lawman makes a mistake, like Bayard did, I dunno, it kind of evens itself out somehow."

"Here's the man you want to succeed you, Mr. Gavin," Hewitt said. "There are too few lawmen who have any feelings left."

Gavin said nothing. Meade Hutton left to spend a lonely night in the sheriff's office, guarding the man who had killed his brother with his chained fist. Gavin, who had eaten very little, refused both coffee and fresh apple pie.

"I'm going to eat pretty light for a few days, Mr. Hewitt. I had a real bad attack of indigestion yesterday," he said apologetically.

Mrs. Gavin bustled about, heating the coffee and filling the sugar bowl. Hewitt waited until she had left the room and then dropped his voice.

"Sure it was indigestion, Sheriff? Sure it wasn't heart?" he said softly.

"I'm sure that's what it was. Third attack I've had. My wife don't know. Only me and Dr. Schickel."

"Why do you hang on, then? You're not broke. You can retire, can't you?"

Gavin looked down at the table. "Got a few things to do first, if I can. This has been a good town to us, Mr. Hewitt. I'd hate to leave it worse off than it was when I took office."

"The State Line Gang, you mean."

"Yes, mostly."

"Don't you think it's time we both showed our hole cards, Mr. Gavin?"

Gavin looked up and met his eyes steadily. "Don't really think you've got one, Mr. Hewitt."

"I might have, and again, you might be right. How about one by the name of McDonald?"

"Mystic?"

"No, I've never heard his first name. Mr. Gavin, nobody can work blindfolded. I've felt all along that McDonald is the shim that keeps this whole mess from falling apart. Who was he? What brought him here? You say he ran off with a tart and committed suicide. His wife stayed. Why? This wasn't her hometown. Had either of them put any money in stock in the bank?"

In a moment, Gavin seemed to wake up. He said, slowly, "I told you about that. McDonald—"

"What was his first name?"

"Forrest, Forrest F. McDonald. He embezzled some money from the bank and—"

"How much?"

"Eight thousand. His wife made it up from the money she inherited from her own family. She—"

Hewitt hit the table with his fist. "Come on, Sheriff Gavin, I wasn't born yesterday. You told me once that he had bought stock in the bank, and that it had become worthless."

"Sure, after he embezzled from it, the stock—"

"How much did he have invested in stock?"

"Why, ten thousand, I believe."

"Do you know if that was all he embezzled?"

"No. When Mystic made it good, there was no crime. Listen, Mr. Hewitt, I went all the way to Macon, Georgia, to see what I could find out about them. No question about it, there was money in both families, and he was a banker and a good one. Porter told me once that, when the bank got big and busy, and he knowed Dick wasn't going to be no help to him, he advertised for a good banker to come in and take charge of things. That's how he got hold of Forrest McDonald. And that's what I heard in Macon. That he quit a good job there for a better one here.

"But I talked to some people that didn't have much use for him. Like they never understood what McDonald knowed about banking that would make him valuable to a bank out here—or anywhere else. Some said he'd growed up in a bank job there because his family was rich, that was all. And yet, as I say, others told me he was just one *hell* of a good banker.

"Now, you tell me, Mr. Hewitt, what a man in my position is supposed to do. Here's the bank claiming that all shortages have been made up by Mystic. Here's the bank examiners, saying the books balance and the bank is sound. Here's Porter Lansing, the biggest man in the county, looking me right in the eye and grinning and saying I'm too good a sheriff to lose. He might as well've said to mind my own business or hunt another job—and he could do it to me, too!"

Hewitt finished the pie and coffee while he thought it over. "If we had any idea how big the embezzlement was, we'd be in a better position to make a judgment."

"How so?"

This man, Hewitt thought, is not that stupid. He may not know banking, but he knows people as well as I, or better . . . He said, "It makes a lot of difference whether you're dealing in dimes or dollars. Many a man can be impeccably honest when it only costs him a few bucks, but when you get up in the thousands, you're getting dangerously close to too many people's price. Here's another touchy question, Sheriff. What shape is Porter Lansing in, financially?"

"You come right at a man with guns blazing, don't you? Well, there was a lot of talk, a few years ago, that Porter had too much money invested in high-priced horses to be solvent. Don't know how much truth there was in it, but one thing is sure—he keeps only about a third as many horses as he used to," Gavin said.

The old sheriff was tiring, a sign that his heart might not be in very good shape after all. Hewitt excused himself, thanked Mrs. Gavin for the supper, and went to Mystic McDonald's house. It was dark, and the fires were banked. There was a note on the table for him, saying that Mystic was spending the evening with Beth Durant and Christine Zollner, and that there were baked beans in the oven that only needed warming up.

Hewitt studied the handwriting on the note for a long time. Mystic McDonald wrote an attractive hand, but it strove for legibility rather than beauty. It was the handwriting of a good accountant, a person of character, one who wanted above all to be understood. No shadings or backslant or other feminine tricks. Just plain, honest writing.

He lighted both kitchen lamps, sat down, and tried to sift the facts in this annoyingly perplexing case. He faced up to one fact, finally—that somewhere, he could smell a big, fat fee for Bankers Bonding & Indemnity Company. This was no act of compassion, no more clearing of a youth unjustly accused. There was money to be made here.

Five minutes after he sat down, there was a knock on the door. It was the chairman of the Board of County Commissioners. The board, he said, had met in special session that evening. On recommendation of Sheriff Arthur Gavin, it had voted unanimously to appoint Jefferson Hewitt acting sheriff until further notice.

"It's not a job I would seek out, but I don't see how I can turn you down, thank you," Hewitt said.

"You're entitled to a full-time deputy, too, you know," said the chairman.

"I'll take Meade Hutton, if we can get him."

The chairman, a grizzled old cattleman who had contested the Ogallalas for his land, nodded with satisfaction. "Kind of hoped you'd say that. He's the man Art would like to have, too, but Art figgered it's up to you to pick your own help."

CHAPTER ELEVEN

But in the morning, when he rode out to Porter Lansing's horse ranch, Meade Hutton did not want to be deputy sheriff. He did not want even to talk about it. "I got a job. It's a better job than deputy," he said.

"Art Gavin wants you to take it," Hewitt said.

"Well, I ain't going to. I'm busy, Mr. Hewitt. I ain't got time to talk to you."

"You mean," Hewitt said, "that Porter Lansing doesn't want you to take the job."

Hutton whirled on him, left fist clenched. "I told you, I'm busy! Now get the hell out of here."

There were always these hidden currents and crosscurrents in any small town, and the ones Hewitt had struggled with were important because they had led to murder and theft and other crimes. He had long ago learned when to push and when to stand aside—when to buck local lines of power, and when to yield. This felt like one of the times to push and buck.

Hewitt said, "If Porter Lansing is unhappy about my being acting sheriff, ask him how he'd like it if I picked one of the Burlington detectives for my deputy. I'm trying to do my job without stirring up any more stink than is necessary. Maybe if I had stirred up more, your brother would still be alive. Maybe if I bring in a Burlington man and stir up a lot of it, we can save some other damn fool's life and—"

Hutton came at him with a speed amazing in so big a man,

pumping with that left like a professional prizefighter. Hewitt had no chance to sidestep. All he could do was go with the punch. It caught him in the ribs under his right arm, and pain screamed through that whole side of his body. He let himself stumble against Hutton, tucking his chin into his shoulder just in time to catch Hutton's hard fast sharp jolting right glancingly on the skull, just above his ear.

His hat brim crumpled under the blow and saved him most of the force of it. He let himself drop to his knees limply, and when Hutton made the mistake of stepping one step backward, Hewitt reached into his hip pocket for his sap and came to his feet and moved with Hutton. His mind was fuzzy and his breath hurt him, and it hurt him to make his right arm take the small, snapping circle with the lead-weighted sap. But he saw the astonishment in Meade Hutton's face just before the sap took him in the forehead, and the face went blank.

He caught Hutton and eased him to a sitting position with his back against the stable wall. Two of the stablemen came out of the bunkhouse and watched him warily. The pain in Hewitt's ribs was easing, but they were going to be sore for a while, and his hand wanted to tremble as he took a cigar out of his breast pocket and lighted it.

The two men watched silently, and time went on and on and on as Hewitt puffed at his cigar. Eventually, Hutton moaned and shivered and moaned again. He opened his eyes blearily. Hewitt waited until he saw them come into focus.

"If you think I'm going to fool around and fist-fight you, Meade, you're stupider than I think you are. Better get up off that cold ground and let's go see Porter Lansing together," he said.

"What did you hit me with?"

Hewitt took the sap from his pocket. "This. And next time, it will be something else you're not looking for. In my job, Meade, they don't pay losers. There's a lot I could teach you about law enforcement, about self-defense, about staying out of fights you can't win. You can use all of that knowledge, when you get to be sheriff."

"You said deputy sheriff."

"How long do you think Art Gavin is going to stay on the job? He's a sick man. You're the man he wants to succeed him. What's Lansing going to think about that?"

Meade carefully got to his feet, staying well out of Hewitt's reach. "I don't know. How would I know? He don't tell me what he thinks."

"Meade, how many horses have you got here now?"

"Forty-three."

"How many did you have a year ago?"

"Oh, about seventy head, give or take a few."

"Two years ago?"

"A hundred or more. Why?"

"Three years ago? He's closing this place up, isn't he? He's selling off horses, and has been for several years, isn't he?"

"That ain't so. He had too many horses here, and a lot of them was only second-rate. You look out there now, and find me one single damn second-rate horse, Hewitt! You won't find this much quality on any horse-breeder's place within a hundred miles, I don't care how many head he's raising."

"Let's go talk to him."

Hewitt smiled as he said it, a smile that said, You have hurt me and I've hurt you. It's a stand-off, and no hard feelings on my part. . . . Meade turned without a word and went into the stable for his saddle.

The trotter, hitched to the racing sulky, stood in front of Howard Junkins' Saloon, held by a frowsy old man who would be grateful for any sum, however small, on a cold and lonely morning. As Hewitt and Meade tied at the hitch rail beside the bright bay stallion, the depot agent came hurrying down the sidewalk toward them.

"Mr. Hewitt, Mr. Hewitt, lucky I seen you. I got a couple of wires for you," he called.

Hewitt excused himself to Hutton to take the wires. The agent waited in case there should be a reply. The first telegram Hewitt read was from his partner, Conrad Meuse. It said:

GEDDIES IN TODAY SAID WATCH YOURSELF THEY ARE ONTO YOU STOP KNOW HE HAS BEEN BELLE FOURCHE STOP IS THIS ANOTHER MACDOUGAL

He handed Conrad's telegram to Meade Hutton to read, while he opened the other one. It was from Joseph E. Burke, president of Jersey Interstate Bonding Corporation, and it said:

YOU ARE HEREWITH AUTHORIZED AND REQUESTED MAKE FULLEST EXAMINATION FARMERS AND MERCHANTS BANK SCHOOL HILL NEBR AND TO CANCEL BOND WITHOUT NOTICE IF YOU DEEM ADVISABLE STOP MR PORTER LANSING BEING ADVISED BY WIRE SIMULTANEOUSLY STOP AWAIT YOUR REPORT WIRE OUR EXPENSE

"I'll probably have a couple of wires to go later in the day," Hewitt said to the agent. "I suppose you have one for Mr. Porter Lansing? I think we'll find him in here, having breakfast."

"I—I just shoved one under the door of the bank for him," the agent replied.

And very wisely indeed, Hewitt thought, watching the man scuttle away. Lansing would not reward the bringer of bad news with a smile, and the agent could not have taken the message from the wire without knowing what was in it.

"I don't get this," Hutton said.

Hewitt took Conrad's wire back from him. He said, "Milt Geddies is an old bank and stagecoach robber. We've been good friends for years."

"I see," Hutton said. "Kind of a chancy friend, I'd say, for a detective."

Hewitt smiled. "Oh, Milt has been reformed for years, too. Apparently he has picked up some talk in South Dakota that worried him enough for him to take the train all the way to Cheyenne to warn me. Know anyone in Belle Fourche?"

"I been there a time or two. I ain't acquainted."

"I imagine it's a town where a few men on the dodge from the law might be able to hole up safely. Kind of a tough town, would you say?"

"Well, yes."

"If they're onto me—whoever they are—it must be because they think I'm onto them."

"The State Line Gang?"

"That's a reasonable inference."

Hutton squinted at Hewitt a long time. "Are you onto them?"

"To an extent. Let's go in and have a bite of breakfast."

Hutton seized his arm as he turned toward the door. "Wait a minute! What do you know that Art Gavin don't know?"

"Nothing."

"Bayard said that Art ain't none too bright. He said the State Line Gang could make him look like a fool. Bayard said—"

"He said too much, Meade, and it was a habit of his, and it got him killed. There's no smarter law officer in the country than Art Gavin, and nobody's going to make him look like a fool."

"Then how do you know more than him?"

"I just told you, I don't," Hewitt said patiently. "I'm only guessing. I'm sure Gavin has made the same guesses. The only difference between us is that I come in from the outside, with no strings on me. I don't give a damn who draws the queen of spades. Art has to live in this town the way it is, not the way he'd like it to be."

He shook off Hutton's hand and went into the saloon. The banker had just finished eating breakfast, and was counting small silver into the bartender's hands. He grinned at Hewitt, and then saw Meade Hutton and scowled.

"What the hell are you doing here, Meade?" he said.

"We'll be over to the bank in a few minutes and explain, after we have eaten," Hewitt said quickly, to save Hutton the embarrassment.

"I ain't going to the bank for a while. I'm going to work my horse a little more."

"I think you'll want to go to the bank, Mr. Lansing. There's an important telegram waiting for you there—damned important!"

Hewitt smiled at him and went past him to the end of the bar. He heard Lansing go out the front door without another word. He heard the ring of the bay stallion's iron shoes and the creak of the sulky as it went spinning away. He looked around at Hutton.

"Hungry? How about a steak and a couple of fried eggs?"

"Mr. Hewitt, I didn't come here to eat. I don't know what this is all about, but let's get to it."

"Come on, order something to eat! I want you to read another telegram before we go see Lansing."

Hutton ordered the same breakfast that Hewitt had ordered. They went to a table in the corner, and Hewitt lighted the big lamp over it. There was a box of poker chips and a pottery ash tray on the table. He pushed the poker chips aside and put his cigar in the ash tray. Hutton sat down slowly, uncertainly.

"I notice you grab the chair facing the door," he said.

"Yes, with a blank wall on two sides of me. It's a good habit to get into, if you're going into the business of law enforcement."

"I ain't."

"Don't decide that yet. Read this."

Hewitt handed Hutton the telegram from J.I.B.C. Hutton read it swiftly, but he waited until the bartender had put their mugs of coffee down before handing it back.

"You mean something is wrong with Porter's bank?" he said, keeping his voice low.

"I have no idea. Obviously, his bondsmen think it is possible."

"Who the hell is that fellow Burke?"

"Meade, anyone in a position of public trust, where he is required to handle the public's money, should be bonded. Do you know what that means?"

"More or less."

"It means that some bonding company agrees to pay off any shortages caused by criminal behavior on the part of the person bonded."

Hutton ignored his coffee. His two big hands made hard fists on the table top. "By God, I'd like to see you look Porter Lansing in the eye, and accuse him of criminal behavior," he whispered.

"If I ever have to do it, I'll look him in the eye. But I'm a bondsman myself. I'm a partner in the firm that bonded Otto Groshardt."

"That son of a bitch! There ain't business enough for two banks in this town, and there wasn't no trouble until he opened up."

"Don't jump to conclusions yet. If you're going to be the sheriff of this county—"

"I ain't. If I didn't know it before, I do now."

Hewitt chuckled. "Just listen and watch and learn, that's all I ask. When the time comes, do what your conscience tells you to do."

Hutton stared off blindly at nothing. "It's hell how fast things can change. Year or two ago, everybody was friends, even with the Dutchman's bank. Now look! Man murdered, now my brother's going to be buried tomorrow, and I almost forgot about that railroad detective being killed. And Art Gavin is sick, and now you're talking about Porter Lansing being a criminal. By God, how fast things can change!"

"Not that fast—and I didn't say Porter Lansing is a criminal! Meade, these things didn't happen that suddenly. Trouble has been a long time coming to this town. I'd like to have your help in clearing it up, so I can go on about my business and you people here can enjoy life again."

Hutton said nothing. The bartender brought their two big platters of food, which they ate in silence. When they had finished and Hewitt had lighted his cigar again, Hutton followed him silently out the door. They led their horses around the corner and down the street to the bank.

Dick Lansing came out of the bank just as they reached for the doorknob. He was pale-faced, and his mouth was grimly taut, but he was able to force a nervous laugh when he recognized them.

"Oh Jesus, what a time for you to show up, Mr. Hewitt! The old man is on a real rampage," he said.

He did not want to linger and gossip, but almost ran on down the street. Hutton held the door open and let Hewitt go in first. There was a woman at the teller's cage, getting her savings passbook balanced. Across the room, Mystic McDonald sat at a corner desk that was neatly littered with papers and a big account book. She had a pencil in her hair, and a scratch pad was at hand. Hewitt could not judge, at this distance and in this light, whether her expression was angry or worried.

At the president's desk, Porter Lansing sat with his tall frame hunched forward. In his hand was the .45 that had been Wes Hardin's gun. It was pointed straight at Hewitt. Behind Hewitt, Meade Hutton let the door close. He saw the gun, and Hewitt heard him step nimbly out of the line of fire.

"You know, Mr. Hewitt, I'm nervous somehow this morning," Lansing said. "You'll never know how close I come to pulling this trigger when you came in there. Why, I might have accidentally shot you dead!"

"I don't see you doing anything accidentally, Mr. Lansing," Hewitt said, walking toward the banker. "I guess you got your telegram. I got the mate to it."

"I don't know what I'm going to do about it, though. You want to pull up a chair? Meade, what the hell are you doing in town with Mr. Hewitt, anyway?"

"I'm the acting sheriff," Hewitt said, before Hutton could answer. "I want Meade for my deputy, and I think Art will want him, too, when he goes back to work. I hope to persuade you that he'll be a lot more valuable to you there than he is on your ranch."

"I don't give a damn." It did not seem to matter at all to Lansing—he did not really bother to think about it. He fingered a telegram from his shirt pocket and dropped it on the desk without unfolding it. "What," he said suddenly, looking up at Hewitt from under shaggy, frowning eyebrows, "do you expect to find in my books, pray tell?"

Out of the corner of his eye, Hewitt saw Mystic's head snap up. He said, "I don't know. I only got the wire myself this morning. What should I expect to find?"

"Nothing." Lansing turned in his chair. "Mystic, come here! Look what we got this morning."

The woman arose and came over to Lansing's desk. He handed her the telegram from Joseph E. Burke, of J.I.B.C. Hewitt glanced at Meade Hutton, and saw him staring raptly at the woman. He had forgotten that anyone else was in the same room.

Mystic read the wire and put it down. "You'll find everything in order, Jeff. We balance, and we're in very good shape in every way," she said serenely.

"I'm sure everything is fine," he said.

There was almost a smile on her lips—almost, but not quite. "What puzzles me is the timing."

"Of what? Of this audit? I have done other investigative work for them, and we have booked quite a few bonds with them."

"But how strange this assignment should come, just when you're here in town!"

She was having fun with him, baiting him in a friendly way, letting him know that she, for one, was not fooled at all. His respect for her rose sharply, and at the same time, it seemed to him that he had never seen a lovelier woman than Mystic at this moment. Her face had a touch of color that made it girlishly beautiful, and under that gray-streaked hair, dramatic in the extreme.

He showed his teeth under his mustache in a smile. "Yes, a remarkable coincidence, perhaps—but again, perhaps not. Have you had any problems with them recently?"

"With the bonding company? No."

"Or with anyone. With the examiners, with your stockholders, even with your accounts. Is there any way you could have come to the attention of the courts, say in a lawsuit alleging fraud or gross negligence? Those things affect your bonding credit."

She looked him straight in the eye. "Nothing of that kind at all. Why would you think that?"

"I don't think it. I mention it as one possibility. They would have no way of knowing where I am. They would have to reach me through my partner in Cheyenne. I'm thinking that perhaps they tried to reach me on something else, my partner told them where I am, and if your bank was already ticketed for an audit, this would be the time to do it."

"We haven't been examined by them in years and years. Perhaps they just think it's time," she said. But her eyes carried a different message, mocking but still friendly. Oh come now, Jeff, they said—you'll have to do better than that. . . .

"When do you want to get at the books?" Lansing said.

"Not soon. I came in here, you know, to fix it up so Meade could be my deputy."

"Oh, are you going to be a deputy sheriff, Meade?" Mystic cried. "Oh, I'm so glad! You'll be very good at it, and I know Art Gavin will be much relieved."

"Thanks, Mystic. Do the best I can," Meade mumbled.

"Come in whenever you want the books, Jeff," said Mystic, turning back to her desk. She took a step or two, turned back suddenly. "How hungry are you going to be for supper tonight? This is a busy day for me, and I thought I'd just put some potato soup on to cook while I work."

Potato soup, he said, would do him fine, and he wondered at the streak of cruelty in one so beautiful, one who had never been anything but kind to him. She had twisted the knife deliberately in Meade with that, and Meade was almost sick at his stomach as they untied their horses. His hand shook, and his eyes were those of a blind man.

"Who will take your place at the ranch, Meade?" said Hewitt.

Meade seemed to come out of a deep, painful trance. "I dunno. I'll have to keep an eye on things until I find somebody for Porter."

"How about Albrecht Raue? He looks like a good, reliable worker to me, and young as he is, I think he could handle a crew. And I know he can handle a horse."

Meade shook his head. "But he's a friend of Otto Groshardt. Them Dutchmen stick together."

"Meade, how much can he help or hinder the business of either bank? Think about it."

"Might work out all right."

"When can you go to work at the courthouse?"

"Day after tomorrow. I'll have a lot to do out to the ranch today, and tomorrow they're burying Bayard."

"I've got a hunch about that. Bayard was pretty well liked. There'll be a big crowd at his funeral, won't there?"

"Oh, sure. Most of the stores are going to close down."

"The banks, too?"

"Oh no, not the banks."

"If you were running the State Line Gang, could you plan a better time to hit a bank here than that? Whoever is running that gang knows this town well enough to know it will be almost deserted during the funeral. What time is it, by the way?"

"Eleven in the morning."

"Can you find me four or five good men to act as temporary deputies until the funeral is over tomorrow? We'll have to get together with them today, and plan how we'll handle it. And you'll have to pay your respects to your brother by doing his job for him then."

"I—I reckon so."

"One thing more." Hewitt took hold of Hutton's coat sleeve and shook his arm gently. "Sometimes instinct is a better guide than manners and morals, Meade. When you feel like slapping a pretty woman down on her pretty butt, don't automatically reject the idea as being unworthy of a gentleman. It may be just what she needs—and wants."

CHAPTER TWELVE

They went down to the courthouse and were sworn in together by Burt Williams, the county judge, who made a little ceremony of pinning their badges on them. This was not the first time that Hewitt had served as a temporary law officer, and he had things to do. The judge's dawdling solemnity got on his nerves, until he saw how it impressed Meade Hutton.

They parted without a handshake. Meade went out to the ranch to give what might be his last orders there, and then to go on the long ride to where Albrecht Raue was working. He promised to be back in town by dark. Hewitt rode past the bank, slowly enough to see through the window and make sure that Mystic McDonald was still there. He tied the horse on the street and then walked swiftly up the road to her house.

She had banked both fires, and the temperature had dropped sharply in it. Hewitt did not fool around. He went straight to her room and stood in the middle of it a moment, studying it. From not far away, he could hear the *chuff-chuff-chuff* of a steam engine and the scream of a circular saw, cutting wood. It annoyed him, since the noise might well prevent him from hearing Mystic, if she came in.

He opened a neat, orderly closet that was full of a musky sachet. A glance convinced him that this was not the place. Where then? What he wanted was probably small, and would be put somewhere so obvious that a searcher would run the risk of overlooking it, holding it in his hand. He

opened the two top drawers of her dresser, and saw it immediately. It was a small handful of old letters, tied with a pink
ribbon, and stored with her perfumes and powders and the
other little, secret stratagems used by a very attractive
woman who had a little—or perhaps more than a little—gray
in her hair.

He untied the pink ribbon carefully, and found what he
wanted in what seemed to be an ancient letter from her
mother. There were four tiny ruled sheets, cut from a ledger
or journal. He chose one with a line that looked familiar.
There was no time to copy it. All he could do was steal it.

He slipped the sheet into his shirt pocket, carefully tied the
letters together again, and hurried back to where he had tied
his horse. Back, then, to the courthouse. There were so many
people wanting to shake his hand—some genuine well-
wishers, many merely curious—that he had to run up the steps
and borrow a small office from the county clerk, where he
could concentrate behind a closed door.

He sat down at a desk and copied, swiftly, the symbols on
the tiny sheet he had abstracted from Mystic's dresser
drawer. He put the original back in his shirt pocket and
leaned his elbows on the table, to frown over the copy. He got
out a pencil and began taking notes. In a few moments, he
had the answer.

He carefully shredded his notes into tiny scraps and threw
them in the waste basket. He thanked the clerk for his courtesy and returned to Art Gavin's office—his office, for the time
being—and motioned to Howard Junkins, who had been left
in charge as a temporary deputy by Gavin. Together, they
walked back into the jail, which consisted of three steel-
barred cells.

One was a large one, with six bunks. The other two con-
tained two bunks each. In the back one, the prisoner who had
killed Bayard Hutton and Jacob Zollner lay on his back on

the bunk, with his hands folded across his stomach. He seemed to be sleeping.

"Caskie," Hewitt said. He had to repeat the name before the prisoner opened his eyes and turned his head.

"Where'd you get that name?" was all he said.

"It will do until you give me a better one."

"I don't have to give you nothing."

"I know that. I just thought you might want to."

The prisoner sat up slowly. He yawned and ran his hands through his heavy shock of white hair. He did not look up at the two men standing just outside his cell. His entire, bulky frame seemed to exude a total despair, not quite a resignation but something close to it. From now on, every moment left would be misery, and the worst one of all would be the final one, when the trap door was tripped and he fell to the end of the rope. It was an attitude familiar to Hewitt, but one that he expected never to get used to.

"Why the hell would I want to do anything for you? You're going to railroad me right to the gallows. A working man ain't got a chance. You and that goddam crooked sheriff and the thieving bankers, all of you are together to keep a poor man down. A man hasn't got a chance against you. You're all a bunch of crooks. If a man won't kiss your hind end, hang him! Why should I want to do anything for you?" he said despairingly.

"Ain't going to do you no good to call the sheriff a crook. Everybody knows better than that," Junkins said, when Hewitt remained silent.

Caskie raised his head and glared at Junkins. "He's the biggest crook of all. How can a man get as rich as him on a sheriff's pay? It can't be done."

"Art Gavin ain't rich."

Caskie merely grunted. Hewitt waited a moment and then said, "You got talked into this, Whitey. I know it and you know it. Now you're sitting here behind bars, waiting to stand trial on two murders. I know who talked you into it. He's capering around, free as a fall colt. He won't even bring you a sack of tobacco, will he?"

The prisoner dropped his eyes to the floor and said nothing. Hewitt went on, not quite as sharply, "If I were in your spot, Whitey, I'd be looking ahead, trying to earn a little mercy. I don't know whether you can or not, but it's worth thinking about."

"Mercy. What the hell mercy is there in spending the rest of your life in the pen?"

"I have known men who made it out. Maybe you haven't got that much guts, Whitey. Maybe you're one of those culls that are born to hang, while your friends go free. I just wanted to tell you that Howard, here, will come get me any time you want to talk to me."

"That'll be never."

"Tomorrow at this time, you know, the brother of the deputy you killed will be in charge here. I'd say that sort of puts a time limit on things."

He nodded to Howard to follow him and went out. The sheriff's office had filled up again, with word that Hewitt was in the courthouse. The yammer of voices came through the door clearly. Junkins, looking embarrassed, motioned to Hewitt to step into the little stone-walled room in the cell block that served as a woodshed. Hewitt went in and closed the door behind them.

Junkins dropped his voice almost to a whisper. "I don't know what you've heard, Mr. Hewitt," he said, "but Art Gavin ain't a rich man."

"I'm sure of that."

"He'll have enough to live on, I reckon, and to keep his wife after he's gone. He—he was in a couple of little land deals, you see . . ."

His voice dwindled away, and Hewitt thought, and I'll bet I know somebody else that was in them with him, Mr. Junkins. . . . He clapped Junkins on the back. "You're always going to hear that kind of talk about a man in public office," he said. "You learn when to take it seriously, and when not to, after a time."

Junkins sighed with immense relief. Together they pushed through the crowded office, Hewitt snatching briefly at hands held out for him to shake. "Thanks, but I'm just keeping the chair warm. You've got a good man in here, and he'll be back. Mighty nice town, and let's try to keep it that way until Sheriff Gavin is on the job again," he told them smilingly as he escaped.

He got his horse out—the horse Art Gavin had loaned him—and rode to the sheriff's stout little house on the other side of town from Mystic McDonald's. There were roads here, not streets. Mystic's neighbors could keep cows and horses, but Gavin also raised two hogs to butcher and three or four to sell.

Mrs. Gavin, a shy woman who must have been a beauty in her time, let him in. "Art's in the kitchen reading," she whispered. "I'm so glad you came, Mr. Hewitt! He gets grouchy when he's sick."

The sheriff had his shoes off, and his sock feet were on the edge of the open oven door. His spectacles were on the end of his nose, and he was so intent on the book he was reading that Hewitt entered entirely unnoticed. But Gavin did not jump with surprise when Hewitt's feet marched into the corner of his vision. His nerves were under control. He closed the book on a bookmark, took off his glasses, and looked up.

"I hear you talked Meade into it," he said. "Pull up a chair."

Hewitt did so, laughing. "Word gets around, doesn't it? Mind telling me who told you?"

"Mystic. No more than two minutes ago."

He had cut it close, then. She might easily have walked in while he was ransacking her dresser drawer. "Sheriff," he said, "is there a lake around here, anywhere close?"

Gavin looked puzzled. "None closer than seventy or eighty miles. You get down close to the sandhills, you find the lakes. All we got around here—well, they call it Borio's Pond."

"I see. One other foolish question. Do you happen to know Mystic McDonald's maiden name?"

"Why, seems I heard it, maybe, but I can't tell you what it is. Why?"

"Would you recognize it if you heard it?"

"I might."

"Would it be Lake?"

Those mean little eyes narrowed slightly. "Yes, it would."

"Do you remember exactly when she and her husband came here?"

"Yes, I do. Nine years ago this month, I think it was the thirteenth."

"Remember when the husband absconded? When he left town?"

Gavin was silent a moment. "I can tell you that exactly. He was here just four days short of five years. I don't want you to make too much of this, Mr. Hewitt. I'm one of them people that remember dates."

"I have a little of that myself. It would be about a year and a half after Otto Groshardt opened the American Eagle Bank."

"Yes. You think there's some connection?"

"An indirect one, at least. Let me show you a couple of wires I just received."

He handed them to Gavin, who did not have to put his

spectacles on again to read them, and who read them quickly.

"What's a MacDougal?" he asked when he had finished.

Hewitt laughed. "My partner has learned to talk in code, to save money on telegrams. Our wire bills are a fright. I once had a case where I speculated a great deal of time and money on the possibility of a big fee. I went into the case as a favor to a friend, expecting no fee at all. I would have been better off to leave it at that, because I got none in the end."

"Well," said Gavin, "is this a MacDougal?"

"I don't know."

"You figger there's something wrong at Lansing's bank?"

"I know there is. I don't know if there are losses, or if there is criminality attached, or if the situation has been corrected. I think we're going to clear Albrecht Raue when we bring Whitey Caskie to trial. That's what I came here to do. I'll get a nominal fee out of J.I.B.C., but not enough to justify a long stay here."

"What would it take to do that?"

"Why—recovery of some missing money. Something like that, where I'm entitled to a percentage of a fairly substantial amount."

"You going to go through Porter's books?"

"Sheriff, don't treat me like a child. If Mystic was here, she told you about my visit to the bank. Now, I wish you'd tell me why she did."

Gavin folded his arms and looked down at the floor. He said carefully, "I've had some dealings with the bank, over the years. I won't say I could have went in there and had them deals if I wasn't sheriff, but there wasn't nothing crooked about them. Mystic figgered I was entitled to know you might be on my neck."

"Let me tell you what kind of deals they were, Sheriff. You knew of somebody selling his place for less than it was worth, or about to lose it on a debt. If some raggedy-ass cowboy heard about it and went in to see Porter Lansing, Lansing would have thanked him and handed him a ten-dollar tip. When Sheriff Gavin went in, Lansing loaned him the money to buy the place."

"Something like that. I paid the same interest anybody else paid. I know a little bit about land values. They never took no risk, nohow. I bought and sold quite a few times. I made money every time, and so did the bank. I got nigh onto eleven thousand dollars in savings, besides this house. If that bank is broke, so am I. If it comes out that I got special favors, I'll never be elected again. If you—"

Hewitt cut in, "Mr. Gavin, let me tell you how I feel about this. In the debates in New York, on the ratification of the United States Constitution, Alexander Hamilton said something that ought to be carved in stone over every courthouse and city hall and legislature in the country. Hamilton was our first—"

"I know who Alexander Hamilton was. Secretary of the Treasury under Washington. Killed by Aaron Burr in a duel. What did he say that's so important?"

Hewitt closed his eyes. "Let's see how close I can come to giving it exactly. He said, 'The great source of all the evils which afflict republics is that the people are too apt to make a choice of rulers who are either politicians without being patriots, or patriots without being politicians.' There may be citizens who would prefer a sheriff who is a damned fool about land values, but I'm not one of them—not so long as he does not steal, sell favors, or otherwise play the fool, whore, crook, bully, or extortionist. If I go into the Farmers and Merchants Bank books, I'm sure I'll learn all about your deals with them. And I'm just about as sure that I'll find that, whatever is wrong with the bank, your deals did not contribute."

Gavin merely nodded, but his eyes betrayed his gratitude. "Any way I can help?"

"Maybe," Hewitt said. "Tell me what you make of this."

He handed the sheriff the copy he had made from the little ruled sheet stolen from Mystic's dresser drawer:

MXMC	CYEXII
YXIE	MASXET
IXYS	TIKXSE
IXYA	SELXCA
LXMI	MMKYXIE
AXSE	KEEXEE
KXT	ACLXLI
KXMK	YEIXKE
MEXMM	TYIXEE
MMXMI	MSIEXEE
MMXYS	YTEIXLE
MMXYK	ILIXEE
MYXMS	SEEXEE
MYXYC	SCCXLL

"What in the *hell* is this?" Gavin asked wonderingly.

"We'll get to that in a minute. You tell me that Porter Lansing found Forrest McDonald through an advertisement."

"Yes."

"Sheriff, are you dead sure that he had never known him—or Mystic—before that?"

Gavin took his time. "I ain't sure, no. Claimed he didn't, but I've had my doubts about that, myself."

"Was he—is he now—sweet on Mystic?"

"You can't prove it by me, Mr. Hewitt. When she first came here—well, I was just scared to death there was going to be a hell of a scandal, that old man was so damn crazy about her. His wife had been dead a long time, and no woman around here could ever get close to him. By now, I'd say, he's over it. She could handle him in that, like she handled him in everything. I told you once before, I've heard that she's ten times the banker he is."

"I see. What kind of board of directors does that bank have?"

"Hell, what kind do you expect? All local people. Mystic's on it. She runs it, same as she runs everything she bothers with. Mr. Hewitt, what *is* this fool list?

"A few more questions, first. Did anyone else ever know about these deals you had with the bank?"

Gavin shook his head. "No, nobody."

"Sure about that?"

"Mr. Hewitt, what's in your mind?"

"How about Jim Sweetland?"

"Oh, hell, a long, long time ago, I bought the Chidister place right out from under Jim's nose. He was sore as hell about it. He tried to jump all over Porter Lansing about it, but that never got him nowhere. He—"

"What was the Chidister place?"

"Couple of side-by-side homesteads to the south of here. They raised good barley, and—"

"Make any money on that deal?"

"Not very much. I let the place go less than a year after I bought it."

"Did Jim Sweetland try to buy it from you?"

"He wanted it, but you've got to understand, Mr. Hewitt, that Jim was a little old three-horse farmer in them days. A half-section of land, nearly two hundred acres under plow, was way too much for him. He—"

"Was he upset when you sold it?"

"I reckon, but he knowed better than to jump me about it. I took less than a thousand dollars of profit out of it. Jim couldn't've raised a thousand dollars to save his soul, and it took eleven thousand cash to swing that deal."

"And you never had words over it."

"Over that or anything else. Jim knowed better. I don't know how he *felt*. But he got the same treatment from me that everybody else got."

"But he did make some money later?"

"Yes, enough to get into debt over his head."

"And he blamed Porter Lansing when he went broke."

"Well, maybe a little. Him and Porter was both horse-crazy, though, and they stayed pretty good friends. Porter let him have money. More money than he should, if what they say is true. He finally had to foreclose on Jim's place. You already knowed that."

"But he still blamed Lansing?"

"No, he blamed Otto Groshardt. He tried to raise money at the American Eagle Bank, to pay off all his debts and save his horses, at least. He knowed he couldn't save the land, but he knowed the price of horses was going to go up. They been pretty low for several years, you know, and he was right, he could've made a lot of money if he could've kept his horses. Like that bay trotting stud Porter bought, O'Malley's Leo. It would've went for about nine hundred, at public sale. Porter paid him twelve hundred and fifty for it, and he could probably get close to two thousand for him now. The British have been buying Army horses, bidding the price up so high that—well, if I's Porter, I'd sell now. These prices can't—"

"Let's get back to Otto Groshardt. Just how does he figure in it?"

"I think Otto came pretty close to letting Jim have the money, but he didn't. I had a deputy then by the name of Tod Bird. He just happened to step into Otto's bank when Jim was hollering and cursing and making all kinds of crazy threats at Otto. Tod was a good, steady head. He got a gun in

Jim's back and walked him outside and disarmed him and sent him home."

"And that ended it?"

"Yes. Jim swore he'd take it out of Otto's hide. In fact, the last time I seen Jim myself, he told me that someday he was going to come back here and fry out Otto's lard until he melted down six or eight thousand. Mr. Hewitt, what are you getting at?"

"Was Sweetland a pretty persuasive man?"

"Oh yes, if you didn't have too much wit. Could talk a badger out of his hole, until you got to know him."

"Whitey Caskie hasn't got too much wit. Any man with his years of experience and his strength has no business being reduced to shooting mink for a living, and robbing old people like the Zollners."

"You trying to tell me you think Jim is head of the State Line Gang?"

"I've thought that ever since his name turned up in that dead man's note."

"But the dead man was one of his gang! Now you seem to think this Caskie is."

"I think he is—now. I hope we can get him to talk before I leave here."

"About what?"

"Where to look for Sweetland."

Gavin glanced down at the little sheet of paper. "What has this got to do with it?"

"I don't know," said Hewitt, "but maybe you can tell me. Listen—"

CHAPTER THIRTEEN

When he took more papers from his pocket, Gavin got up and led the way to the kitchen table. They pulled up chairs, and sat down together. "Remember that first bit of code I showed you?" Hewitt said. "This is what it looked like, if you recall."

He penciled in the letters from memory:

CXYE YMIIXAE TCEXYI

"I thought I knew what it was then," he went on. "I also thought I had a pretty good idea of what it was trying to say. I know I do now. It's a pricing code, Sheriff. Know what that is?"

"No."

"When a storekeeper is putting price tags on his merchandise, he likes to keep track of the cost, too. But he doesn't want the customer to know that cost; so he gets himself a ten-letter combination of words that is easy to remember, and makes those letters serve for the numerals one to zero, or ten. The first pricing code I ever knew about, on the first case I worked when I was with the Pinkertons, the merchant used his wife's maiden name, Belinda Roy. No two letters are the same in that; so each letter can stand for a separate number.

"Say he buys something that costs him fifty cents each, and he wants to sell it for ninety-five cents. The fifth letter in 'Belinda Roy' is *N*, and the last one, for zero, is *Y*. So he marks the price tag this way—"

Hewitt wrote down the symbols, NY/95¢. He went on, "You've seen this many a time, I'm sure. When the merchant wants to put this stuff on sale, he doesn't have to go back to his books to know the cost. Or if he wants to give someone a quantity discount, or favor a friend, he knows how far he can cut without losing money."

"I've seen that before, yes, and never knowed what it meant," Gavin said. "You could send all kinds of code messages this way, I reckon."

"Only numerical data, with this simple a code. The thing that jumped out at me on that first line was that it had only letters in the word 'Mystic,' maybe because she was on my mind. She had dropped the memo, you recall."

"There's an 'X' in it, one in each group of letters," Gavin pointed out.

"Forget X. It's a decimal point or hyphen or some other mark of separation. When I got these other notations, all I had to do was take out the letters in 'Mystic,' and I had 'Lake.' That's why I asked you if there was a lake around here. When you said there was none, that's why I asked you Mystic's maiden name. And when you face up to the fact that Mystic and Porter are the two using this code, it kind of makes you wonder if they didn't know each other when that was her name."

Those mean eyes narrowed. "Go on."

"This is what the key to this pricing code looks like—" He pointed to the lines on the paper:

M Y S T I C   L A K E
1 2 3 4 5 6   7 8 9 0

"Using that key, this is what you get out of that first bit of code we found," he went on, pointing to the next line on his work sheet:

CXYE   YMIIXAE   TCEXYI
6–20   2155.80   460.25

"June the twentieth," Gavin murmured, "and two chunks of money, right?"

"Right! We know that Mystic lost this near the end of last June. We know that was in Porter Lansing's printing. What we want to find out now is whether Lansing sold anything—probably horses—about that time. Do you remember anything, or am I going to have to go after him and pull his teeth?"

"Last June," Gavin said softly. He tilted his chair back on two legs and locked his hands behind his head. He went on dreamily, "June, June. It was May thirteenth I went to Broken Bow to bring back those two little bastards in that stabbing. Why yes, yes. When I got back, that damn stupid Bayard had went off and left Shorty Gamble in charge of the office, to deliver some horses for Porter. Eleven head, nine in Rushville and the other two at some cow outfit on east in Cherry County."

"Pretty good horses?"

"For the average man, yes. As far as Porter was concerned, culls."

"This would average out about two hundred and thirty-seven dollars a head, give or take a few dollars."

" 'Bout right. Port gave Bayard fifteen dollars for delivering them and I gave him pure-D hell. Mr. Hewitt, what does all this add up to?"

"When you take this long coded list I brought you today, and break it down into numbers, it comes out looking like this."

Hewitt brought out the work sheet that showed the uncoded numerals:

1–16	$ 620.55
2–10	183.04
5–23	459.30
5–28	307.68
7–15	1,192.50
8–30	900.00
9– 4	867.75
9–19	205.90
10–11	425.00
11–15	1,350.00
11–23	2,405.70
11–29	575.00
12–13	300.00
12–26	366.77
TOTAL	$10,159.19

"I can see your figures, and I believe them," Gavin said, "but I don't know what they mean."

Hewitt said, "They mean that either Porter Lansing and Mystic Lake are keeping track of money taken *out of* the bank, or they're keeping track of money put *back into* the bank. There are about seven of these sheets. I'd have to decode them and add them up to be sure, but my best guess is that they add up to pretty close to sixty or seventy thousand dollars. And they go back to a year or two *before* Forrest McDonald absconded."

"You think that Porter and Mystic was robbing the bank, and Forrest got onto it and skipped with some himself?" Gavin looked not just bewildered, but suddenly old and sick. His hand trembled on the table. His face had gone gray.

"The evidence might point that way," Hewitt said, "but I don't believe it."

"Why not?"

"I have met a few thieves in my time. So have you. Do you think Mystic McDonald is a thief?"

The old sheriff rubbed his face as though it had gone numb. He did not meet Hewitt's eyes. "I tell you, Mr. Hewitt, if she turned out to be crook-oh, it would just about make me sick of the whole goddam world. But that woman could look you in the eye and tell you the world is flat, and you'd believe it."

"I don't think I would. I live right in the same house with her, and I think that she and I understand each other pretty well. Let's assume that she's honest. Let's go a little farther and say that she's more than honest—she is smarter than a good bird-dog, too, and—you said it yourself—a better banker than her boss."

Those mean eyes narrowed again, and Gavin seemed to get some of his color back. "Then what?"

"Let's say this old fool of a Lansing got into trouble with his bank. We don't know what kind. Maybe bad investments, maybe bad loans. Or some bigger bank sold him some bonds they wanted to get rid of. Just bad judgment, because while I think Lansing may be a fool, I don't think he's a crook."

"I don't think so, either."

"Say he finds himself in a jackpot without a pair—say he knew Mystic when she was Mystic Lake—knew she had banking background somehow—how he might wish he had her here! Maybe it was coincidence that he got her husband—maybe he advertised, knowing the kind of banker her husband was—any way it happened, he got McDonald here to steer him out of his troubles.

"It wouldn't take him long to see that Forrest McDonald would add to his problems, rather than reduce them. Or maybe Mystic warned him. Let's say there's about a fifty-thousand-dollar-shortage, due to Lansing's bad judgment rather than criminality. Mystic shows him how to start liquidating his horses and feeding the money back into the bank. We're assuming, now, that he's putting his own money in to save the stockholders and the depositors. Does that sound like him?"

Gavin thought it over. "He's one tough old bird. He's got money in trust in an Omaha bank, to make sure Dick never has to go hungry. He could foreclose on you without shedding one goddam tear, but if Mystic worked on him, he'd do as she said. And he could slide fifty thousand into the pot without skipping a heartbeat."

"Only," Hewitt said, "they had her husband on their hands, and he could keep books in a bank himself. He was, I take it, that much of a banker, wasn't he?"

"Yes. So he dipped into the cash himself and ran off with his lady friend, and left Porter and Mystic to make up that loss, too."

They were silent a moment. It pleased Hewitt to see how much better Gavin looked than he had just moments ago. Gavin slid the work sheet closer to him and squinted at it. Hewitt ran his finger down the columns.

"Nice chunk in January, see? Not so good in February, and not a cent in March and April. That's why I would say they've been liquidating horses. There's not much cash market for blooded horses in those months. But look, two sums in May, over seven hundred dollars—none in June, but over eleven hundred in July and an even nine hundred in August," Hewitt said.

"September through November—those are the months where we see the big sums—and that's when people have sold their crops and can buy good horses. Over six hundred in December, but my guess would be that these are payments made on earlier fall sales."

"Must seem strange to you, Mr. Hewitt—tracking down a

banker who is putting the boodle back, instead of taking it out."

"Things like this happen, Mr. Gavin. There are people like Whitey Caskie, sure enough. But there are quite a few who aren't."

"We know that some of these State Line toughs have been through here," Gavin said thoughtfully. "If you're right about Jim Sweetland, he'd know about Porter selling off his horses. We damn sure know that they made mighty free with Porter's place. They used it like a branch office. Mr. Hewitt, you can't tell me that Porter don't suspect Jim Sweetland!"

"I've wondered about that myself. One thing bothers me. How close were Dick Lansing and Sweetland?"

"Jim kind of favored Dick, and Dick would like anybody that wasted time on him. But you don't think he's in with that gang, do you?"

"No, but I think his father may think it. That may be why he shies away from pointing the finger at Sweetland—afraid he'll involve his own son."

"What is it you want from me?"

"You know Sweetland and you know this country. Where would he be hiding out, if he was pulling his gang together to raid one or both of these banks?"

Gavin squinted thoughtfully a long time, chewing the idea over in his mind. He shook his head. "I just don't know. Why are you so sure he'll hit here?"

"He'll think all that horse money is in Lansing's bank. He knows we're getting close to him, because we've got Whitey Caskie in jail. We know they're short of money to eat on, or Caskie wouldn't have robbed the Zollners—he wouldn't be sniping at mink. They haven't got forever. If I were in Sweetland's place, and I knew about the funeral of a popular deputy sheriff tomorrow, I'd figure it was now or never."

The sheriff's right hand strayed to the pulse in his own left.

He knew that heart of his by now. His mean little eyes had a burn in them as he said, "You'll have to tell Meade what to do. He's got all the guts he needs, and him and Bayard was always crack shots. But he ain't got much confidence in his own judgment. That's going to come to him, but it won't do you no good tomorrow."

Hewitt stood up, smiling, and picked up his hat. "By tomorrow night, he may be a veteran police officer. Some kinds of showdowns age a man fast."

He went to Junkins' Saloon for a sandwich and a piece of pie, delaying his return to the house as long as possible. Back to the office then, to relieve Junkins so he could eat. He cleared the office with a friendly but sharp warning: "Can't make this a clubhouse, boys. I've let you swarm here, but now it's back to your own hives." When they had straggled out, he tacked a sign on the door: COME IN ON BUSINESS ONLY—THIS IS A BUSY PLACE! YES, THIS MEANS YOU, TOO.

The two railroad detectives, Barney Fels and Neal Evanson, hurried in to say good-by before catching a train out of town. Just when he needed them, they were being summoned back to report to their division chief, but that was life for a railroad dick.

He locked the door behind them and went through the door to the cellblock. There was no indication that Whitey Caskie had moved, and he did not look around when Hewitt came to the bars.

"Tomorrow is the funeral of that deputy sheriff you killed, did you know that?" Hewitt said.

"Funeral of that old Dutchman you claim I shot, too. Both at the same time. According to you, that's all I am, just a murderer," Caskie said.

"Yes, and a mighty poor specimen at that. You know what I think is going to happen tomorrow?"

"What?"

"I think that while those funerals are going on, Jim Sweetland and his renegades are going to hit here and try to rob a bank. Maybe both banks. You know him and I don't. Does that sound like the way his mind would work?"

Caskie said nothing. Hewitt let him think it over a moment and then went on:

"They're going to miss you, Whitey. You'd be a big help in a bank raid, as strong as you are, and the way you can shoot. Of course, you haven't got much guts, but you can get excited enough during a bank robbery to carry you through. But Sweetland isn't going to miss you enough to bust you out of here. You know that, don't you?"

"I don't even know what you're talking about."

"Because you're too stupid to think. All right, try to imagine how you're going to feel tomorrow, when they hit the bank here, and you hear all the shooting, and then have to lie here and listen to them ride out of town. Or what it's going to be like when we stuff a few of them in these other cells. Because I'm going to be staked out for them like Apaches, and there's nothing you can do about it, is there?" Hewitt said.

"When we sprawl all over them, they won't know what hit them. But when they have time to think it over, and see you here in a nice, warm cell, not a mark on you, they're going to think that you talked like a gentleman, aren't they? That we didn't even have to coax you. That you just blab-blab-blabbed everything you knew."

Caskie rolled over and stood up in one powerful motion. He came to the bars and put his face between two of them. He might have got his big hand through, to make a grab at Hewitt or his gun, but he did not.

"What makes you think they're going to raid tomorrow, detective?" he asked.

Hewitt said nothing. He could almost smell the fear and hatred in the man—fear of hanging, fear of being abandoned by his friends—hatred of the whole world, but most of all of police officers.

"How do you know that?" Caskie said. "I sure as hell don't know it."

"No, because that decision wasn't made until after you killed Zollner and Hutton. It's the funerals, man—the funerals that make the difference, can't you see that?"

A big forefinger came between the bars to jab Hewitt in the chest. Caskie's voice dropped almost to a hoarse whisper. "Last fall, Lansing sold six horses to a man by the name of Prudhomme, in Sheridan county. It was our money that paid for them. Prudhomme knowed we was in on a couple of jobs. He wanted in. Damn yella sneaking bastard—"

"Forget him! Prudhomme's dead anyway," Hewitt said, making a guess that was not altogether a guess. Men like Sweetland and Caskie knew what to do about ambitious but unreliable men like Prudhomme.

"Yes," said Caskie, "but he's got a place northeast of here that Jim can use. I don't know how to tell you to get to it, but somebody around here would know. It used to be the Bal-linger place. It ain't much, from what I hear, but there's a shanty and a roof for the horses, and there's feed. Six dark horses. The white points will be dyed. Everybody's been growing a full suit of whiskers. Everybody's carrying a change of coats and hats, so they can shave and change after they split the money. Everybody goes his own way, then. You know what I think, detective?"

"No, what do you think?"

"I think Jim Sweetland is crazy as a bedbug. He has to do all the planning himself. You just have to take orders from the old son of a bitch. He'd just as soon shoot you down as

not. That's what he done to Prudhomme, just shot him dead
across a campfire."

"Not like you did Jacob Zollner, you mean."

The big man flinched hard. He rolled his eyes and clutched
the bars as though to keep from falling down. "You can't
prove I done that," he said, when he could say anything.

"The hell I can't."

"Well listen, detective, I told you all I know about Sweetland. I couldn't stay around him very long, or me and him
would've shot it out. And he don't care whether he eats or
not. A madman, detective! And if they think they're going to
skip out of here and not even get me a lawyer—why they'd've
starved if I hadn't hunted meat for them—and old Jim goes to
California and starts a horse farm while I hang. Is that fair?
Is that fair?"

"If what you have told me is any help to us in rounding
them up, I'll see that the judge knows about it. One more
question. Were you along when they raided the train and
tried to lynch Albrecht Raue?"

"Yes."

"You know that we know why you did it, don't you?"
Again Caskie flinched; and Hewitt went on, "To shift the
blame for the murder of that fellow behind the bank from
you to Raue. Why did you kill that fellow, Whitey? What did
Sweetland say about it?"

Caskie did not hesitate. "I wasn't riding with Jim then. I
run into this fella outside of town here a piece, and rode in
with him. I seen he kept trying to get rid of me, like he was
carrying something he was afraid I'd take away from him. I
tied and follered him on foot, and seen him head straight for
the bank."

Caskie paused to try to remember. One more odd killing—why should that stick in a busy man's mind? "So," said
Hewitt, "with a storm coming on, you saw your chance and

you took it, and the five hundred dollars. Did Sweetland ever find out about it?"

"No."

"Know who the fellow you killed was?"

"Oh, sure. No-good, worthless son of some rich bastard back in Philadelphia. There's a reward for anybody that can tell what became of him, detective. His name—let me see—Wendell something or other. I knowed him in Kansas, see, and he told me all about it. If you got that reward—listen, whoever buried him would see a scar on his head, just behind his ear, that he wore his hair long to cover up—that would prove it, and if you got a reward out of it, why do you have to try me on that one?"

"You're a peach, Whitey," Hewitt said.

He took his time to go through Gavin's desk in the office, and sure enough, there it was, buried about halfway down a stack of dusty old posters and circulars. For information as to the whereabouts of Wendell Hart Crowinshield . . . heart-broken parents solicit assistance all officers . . . reward of Two Thousand, Five Hundred Dollars . . .

He also found Sheriff Gavin's notes on the murder case. The dead man fit the description, even to "short, wide, thick, raised scar about one and one-quarter-inch thick behind left ear." Gavin, Hewitt concluded, was a thorough, methodical officer. All he lacked was a touch of avarice.

CHAPTER FOURTEEN

It looked like a squadron of cavalry, the same grimly competent look, even the same cocksure tilt to the leader's head. However modest Meade Hutton might be in other things, at this moment he knew he was as good as he had to be. He had mobilized twenty-one well-mounted and well-armed men, and there was no question as to who commanded.

The only one Hewitt recognized was Albrecht Raue, riding the poorest horse of all, although he was no more ill dressed than some of the others. Hewitt was headed for home—Mystic's house—when they came down the street from the north, horses jinking against tight reins, strung out in a loose single file for maximum effect. Hewitt could not help smiling broadly as he pulled his own horse down to await them. It was hard not to salute.

"By God, Meade, you're in shape to declare war," he said.

"You said get you some good men. I've still got a few friends around here," Meade replied.

"I reckon you have!" Hewitt looked from man to man, all down the line, before turning back to Meade. "First, we've got to talk—not just you and I, but all of us together. Where can we do that?"

"Livery stable."

"Good! Put your horses up there, and have them fed. I'll tell Howard Junkins to feed everybody as soon as he can. Then let's all get together in the stable in about an hour and a half. I think I've got some news for you."

Meade turned in the saddle to look at his men. No one objected. Hewitt pulled his horse back to let them file past him. He said nothing, even to Albrecht, but he let his face show how he felt. The last man was a wiry little man, shabbily dressed and with a month's growth of graying whiskers. He had a merry, tough face and a pair of sharp, black eyes.

"County's paying for all of this, I s'pose," he said.

"If the county won't, I know somebody who will. Just say charge it," Hewitt replied.

"Suppose they won't?"

"Oh pshaw, who is going to argue with this bunch? Anybody does, tell them that Hewitt's signing the bills."

The little fellow winked, and the file rode on down the street. Hewitt pointed his horse up the hill. Halfway up, he saw a woman ahead of him, carrying a small gunny sack over her shoulder. Bent under the load, she walked slowly but she still carried herself with a grace that he was sure he recognized.

It was Beth Durant. He dismounted, took the gunny sack on his own shoulder, and handed her the reins of his horse. Beth was in a plain and probably old dress, wearing a short, warm jacket and a fur hat. The cold had given her face a high color and her eyes a sparkle that made her beautiful, not just pretty, and the thick jacket could not mask the full lines of her magnificent bust.

"What in the world is in the bag, Miss Durant?" he said.

"Can't you remember my name?" she countered.

He smiled, and she seemed satisfied without an answer. She rushed on, "I have an aunt in Louisiana who sends me pecans every winter—not this many, though, as a rule. I needed the walk—I haven't been out of the house, really—but had no idea it would be so heavy. I'm taking them to Mystic's place. I'm going to live with her after Christine leaves."

"Oh, Mrs. Zollner is leaving town?"

"Yes, going back to a job in Wisconsin. She has to live, you know."

"Didn't her husband leave her anything?"

"He meant to, but he didn't have time to change his will. It all goes to a couple of nephews in the Old Country."

And for this, Hewitt thought, we can thank Whitey Caskie. . . . "What will become of the dog?" he said.

"I'm learning to handle him. I never thought I could, but one can do anything one has to, I find. And we'll be glad to have him, Mystic and I." She shivered. "I'm afraid this town will never be the same again."

"That's not true, and you know it. Towns change. Times change. But people heal, too, and so do towns."

"No, Mystic says something is gone from School Hill that can never come back."

"Innocence, but innocence never lasts forever. I can show you many a little town, just as pretty as this from a train window. You'd think it beautiful, passing through, but there are running sores of hatred and discontent and dishonesty everywhere, and you can't keep on running. You've got to stop somewhere, and either make a place for yourself or own up to your own failure."

"That's easy for a man to say!" she said bitterly.

"Mystic's not running away from it, is she?"

"No, but she's part of it. Of the town, I mean. She has something to live for here." Her voice and her expression had suddenly become passionate and wild. "What is here for me? I'll never forget Jacob lying there on the ground, dead! Such a peaceful, happy house—and then, suddenly—"

She choked up. He was sure she expected him to say something comforting, something reassuring. Well, let her reach her own conclusions, let her face her own problem, perhaps for the first time in her life. They came to Mystic's house, and he put the bag of pecans down to tie the horse to a tree. He shouldered the bag again, and Beth went ahead of him to open the door.

"Mystic," she cried, as she went inside.

There was no answer. She stepped aside to let him come in, murmuring something about the kitchen. She closed the door while he walked ahead and put the bag down in a corner of the kitchen, next to the wood box. Beth called again.

"Mystic! I'm back. Where are you?"

Afterward, he could not remember whether Beth came all the way to him, or if he took a step to her. She came into his arms and threw her own arms strongly around his neck. She kissed him, rather than he, her. Her full, warm lips smothered his hungrily, and he would not have been the man he was had he not kissed her back. He felt her whole sumptuous body pressing against him with the same wild, searching abandon.

"Oh God, Jeff, don't ever leave me, don't go away without me. You're my hope, my soul, my last dream. Oh Jeff, Jeff, can't you love me a little?" she babbled, mouth to mouth.

She stopped kissing to lean her face on his chest, and he disengaged himself expertly before she knew what he was doing. He had an inclination to tremble, but he knew better than to let her suspect how strongly she had shaken him. He felt in his pocket for a cigar, and found that she had crushed all three slightly. He used his fingertips to smooth one out.

"Beth," he said, "you're talking like a damn fool, you know."

"Jeff!"

"You're not a schoolgirl. That kind of talk is unbecoming in a grown woman. And don't look so stricken. You gambled, and you knew the odds were against you. If you didn't know I wasn't a man to settle down and marry on two hours' acquaintance, Mystic would put you wise. Let's not embarrass each other more."

"I—I didn't say anything about marriage."

He smiled at her, a little mockingly. "No? The farthest thing from your mind, I imagine."

"God damn you!"

"Get it out of your system. Beth, there will be other men. Don't give up so easily! How long have you known me? How much time have we spent together? Are you going to nominate yourself a success or failure on the basis of a couple of hours of propinquity?"

"The last time," she said, almost in a whisper, "it was two years and two months. A lifetime! I—I never held anything back. But he—he—how can I say it?"

"He was married." She turned fiery red, but she nodded and met his eyes. He laughed and went on, "These things happen, Beth, but don't try to tell me you held nothing back."

"Oh, I did—I did!"

"Then why is there so much of you left? How old are you, anyway? All right, you don't have to answer. But you never gave up a lifetime to that fellow. I think you got as much out of it as he did. You're not a betrayed and ruined girl. You're a grown woman who went into it with your eyes open and—"

The back door opened, and Mystic came in with her arms full of half-dried, half-frozen clothes from the line. "It's starting to warm up, and it's going to turn to snow before morning," she said, before she noticed the strain between them.

There was a moment of silence, an embarrassed tableau that Beth broke with a sound that was half sob, half laugh. Hewitt would have bet that Mystic would be equal to any situation; and she was indeed.

"I walked in on something, I see," she said. "Should I go out again?"

"You came in at exactly the right moment," said Hewitt. "I'm the sort of stag who seems to bring out the worst in women. Beth, for instance. And I can't stay and talk. She'll tell you about it, Mystic. You tell her what every girl should know, after I'm gone. Is Porter Lansing still at the bank?"

She blinked. "That's a fast change of subject, but no, he isn't. Why?"

"I want to leave a couple of men in the bank overnight. Can you give me a key, or am I going to have to run him down and get his?"

"Why are you—what do you mean, a couple of—I don't understand at all, Jeff."

"We're going to be held up, one bank or both. Maybe today, maybe tonight, certainly not later than tomorrow during the funerals. I've got a small army standing by to make sure it doesn't work. I want to put two in each bank overnight, and I want to keep as many as I can of the bank employees out tomorrow until it's over, so no more will be killed or hurt."

"My God, I can't let you have a key for that! Who would you leave inside?"

"I don't know. Meade Hutton will pick the men."

Her eyes narrowed a little, and her lovely mouth became firm and somewhat straighter. "I don't think I would trust his judgment. Meade is a good horseman, but—"

"I don't think you have any choice, Mystic. I want a large-scale map of the county, too—one that I can take to a meeting. Have you got one?"

"We have a county atlas in the bank, a set of county surveyor's maps, but—"

"Just what I want! Can you get them for me?"

She looked angrier, and lovelier too. Hewitt was aware that Beth was watching them both, and he wished he knew what was going on in her mind. Mystic put the damp, cold clothes on a kitchen chair, obviously using the little job to give her a chance to collect her wits.

"Jeff, aren't you being a little high-handed?" she said. "I'm sure you know what you're talking about when you say we're going to be held up, but need you take charge quite so officiously?"

"It's time someone did. This has dragged on too many years."

"What has dragged on?"

He took from his pocket the little coded sheet with her own neat printing on it, that he had taken from her dresser. She paled a little as she recognized it, but her poise was unshakable.

"Where did you get this, Jeff?"

"You know where I got it."

"Christ, what nerve!"

"Yes, ma'am, all the nerve I need."

"Jeff, it doesn't mean what you think it means. I'm taking it for granted that you broke my silly little code."

"Yes, I did, and I know what it means. I don't jump to conclusions, Mystic, and I have audited other banks and untwisted other people's twisted minds. I'm going into your books soon, and get the figures to a cent. But in general terms, I already know what happened."

"What do you think happened?"

He raised his eyebrows at Beth, meaning, In front of her . . . ? Mystic ignored the warning. He said, "When and where did you know Lansing first?"

"That has nothing to do with it."

"I'm afraid it does, but let's skip it because I haven't got all day. He hired your husband because he wanted you here, didn't he?"

"I grew up in banks, Jeff. I knew more about banking when I was sixteen than Porter does now. I met him in Washington, when I was exactly sixteen. My father was presiding over a convention of bankers, one of those foolish attempts to force Congress to give us stronger banking laws. I kept the minutes. My father was a good banker, but he—"

She fell silent, lost in memories. He said, "But he kept hoping for more from human nature than he ever got out of it, you mean."

"Yes. I was more realistic. Anyway, Porter used to write to my father about the laws. He was a fighter, a romantic fighter. He always asked about me. Well, they paid him off."

"The big banks."

"Yes. Sold him French and Bohemian bonds that they knew would be defaulted."

"And he was too easy on his loan policy, and too many people talked him into too many things. How bad were things when you came here?"

"Almost a hundred thousand dollars."

He whistled softly. "How did he get in touch with you?"

"Wrote letters for two years, and then advertised for a bank manager. I saw the ad, and got my husband to answer it. I'm sure you know the rest."

"How close did you come to getting back to solvency? You surely didn't have access to that much money, even if you put everything he owned as well as everything you owned into the pot."

She said serenely, "Oh, it was much worse before I got hold of things! A hundred and forty-four thousand, but we didn't have to find that much. I wrote a few letters, and offered to go East to negotiate on the bad European bonds. That turned out to be unnecessary."

He laughed delightedly. "They bought them back?"

"Ninety thousand dollars' worth."

"Mystic, you're a wonder!" he said, putting his hand on her shoulder.

She did not try to shake the hand off, but she showed clearly that she did not like it. "Tell me, Jeff, when did you get onto what was wrong—and how? Because we're solvent now, and the books will prove it."

"I never was fooled. I knew Lansing for an old bluffer, a credulous old easy-mark, the first day I was in the bank. Hardin's gun."

"I don't understand."

"He's got a forty-five. Wes Hardin may have used a forty-five a time or two in his career, but he made his name with an old Frontier forty-four. They say he killed forty-three men in his lifetime. I got pretty well acquainted with him. He was a cold-blooded, self-centered, short-tempered troublemaker and there was nothing gallant or romantic about him. Yet he could get sentimental tears in his eyes when he recalled that old forty-four. He himself didn't know how many men he had killed, but he choked up when he told me that that first gun saved his life eleven times.

"By that, he meant that he killed eleven men before any of them could kill him. Good lord, anyone who can think of him as a fighting man to admire hasn't the judgment to run a bank. And when he lets some confidence man sell him a gun out of a pawnshop for Hardin's own, I just wonder that he held onto his bank and his ranch until you could get here to save them for him."

"Jeff, many a fine country bank has been built by men just as ignorant as Porter. They may not know finance, but they know land, people, crops, livestock. This country has been built by bankers who did not want to be bankers—who *had* to be bankers because nobody else—"

"I know," he cut in, "and I've met so many of them! Some became good bankers. Others went broke, and broke a lot of other people with them. And others got good bankers in to

save their hides in time. I'm not trying to tell you anything
about banking, Mystic, but please don't lecture me, either."

She smiled and suddenly they were friends again. She went
to her room and came back with a pair of keys on a heavy,
well-worn brass chain. "This is the upper lock and this is the
bottom one. You won't need to get into the vault, surely."

"No."

"The maps are in the cabinet behind my desk. Is there
anything else I can do?"

"Yes. Stay in the house, both of you. Get Mrs. Zollner
over here, too. Keep that brute of a dog in the house, and if
anyone knocks on the door, make sure you know who it is
before you open it."

"Oh my God," Beth moaned. "Can't you go with us to
bring Christine?"

He raised his eyebrows at her as he went out. Before he
closed the door, he heard her say hotly, "Jeff, you are so
damn maddeningly superior, no woman could stand you!"
She's right, he thought, untying his horse. It's a lonesome
life I lead. . . .

CHAPTER FIFTEEN

He caught Otto Groshardt as he was locking the bank to go home. The German was not happy with the idea of leaving two men in his bank overnight, but he liked even less the idea of being surprised by robbers. He could not resist one sarcastic comment before starting to walk home through the evening's first snow.

"It seems you forget why you came here, isn't it, Mr. Hewitt? All this time, what about poor Albrecht? You smell the reward, you forget Albrecht, eh?"

"Just about, I'm afraid," Hewitt replied. "I hope you'll stay away from the bank tonight unless we call you. And make sure it's us, in case anyone does come after you."

"Make sure what?"

"If I send anyone for you in the night, he'll use the code word *'Nachtdenker.'* If he can't give the password, fire from the hip."

"I think you are a *Nachtdenker.* Maybe tonight, I be one too."

"A lot of us will be." They nodded pleasantly and parted. Hewitt let them get a good fifty feet apart before calling back, "By the way, Otto—I almost forgot. Al Raue is one of the guards tonight, wearing a special deputy's badge."

Nachtdenker—night thinker. He was fairly sure that Otto would get the significance of it. Conrad Meuse had often called Hewitt a night thinker, not exactly as a compliment.

Hewitt knew other Germans who were familiar with the appellation.

He walked toward the livery stable leading his horse, something nagging at his mind. He was not worried about the State Line Gang and Jim Sweetland. He had dealt with enough outlaws to know how their minds worked. He was convinced that stick-up men had to be very good, very smart, and also very lucky, to succeed. They had to do everything right, and then run like rabbits.

The law, on the other hand, could make mistake after mistake, but so long as it did one thing right, it was a cinch to win. He had an excellent mental picture of Jim Sweetland, that quarrelsome, bullying and yet grotesquely self-pitying old failure, who now imagined himself to be a big bandit chieftain. He had been a failure at everything he had ever tried to do. Why should he now hope to succeed at the far more difficult game of robbery?

As for the culls and misfits, the outcasts and grudge carriers and cowardly louts he could recruit, they were even less a problem. Whitey Caskie was probably the pick of the crew—and look where Whitey was, and what had landed him there.

No, he scolded himself, there are just too damn many women in this case. . . . Hewitt liked women, and he did not gloat in the fact that they usually liked him. He knew the advantage that a well-heeled stranger in a fairly romantic role always had over the steadiest of home-town boys. He had conscientiously avoided being the answer to many a small-town maiden's prayer—and yet the presence of an attractive woman was always distracting.

Two of them, two like Mystic and Beth, were poison.

A sullen crew of cowboys awaited him in the livery barn. They had come here for action, and had been forced to stay in the stable, stone sober, for far too long. Sheriff Arthur

Gavin came in not two minutes after Hewitt. He looked fit and he looked calm.

"Mr. Hewitt is still the acting sheriff, boys," he said, as the cowboys who knew him clustered around him. "I'm just here to watch how a big-city detective does things. Go right ahead, Mr. Hewitt. You're the boss."

Hewitt got up on a box to speak to them. He told them of his plan to leave two men in each bank tonight, with two more hidden somewhere on the street where they could keep an eye on each bank. The two on the street would stand one-hour watches, and Meade Hutton would tell the relief men what route to take to the sentry post.

"I don't expect we're going to have any luck tonight. If it hadn't snowed, I think we'd have had a fifty-fifty chance to spring the trap on them sometime before daylight. Just in case they don't show up, either tonight or tomorrow, I've got one more idea. I want you boys to stay here with Meade, while he makes out the watch list. I'll be back in a minute," he said.

Gavin followed him out the door and through the snow to the Farmers and Merchants Bank. Hewitt told him as much as he could about his plans, and was grateful that Gavin did not raise hairsplitting objections or ask foolish questions. Gavin knew as well as Hewitt that what they did was largely up to Jim Sweetland.

Rather than strike a match, Hewitt found the right keys for the right keyholes by feel. They slipped into the dark bank, and Gavin waited by the unlocked door while Hewitt groped his way to Mystic's desk. He found the maps and came back. They locked and tried the door, and returned to the stable.

Hutton had already tolled off the men he wanted in each bank, and the first watch on the outside. Hewitt let Gavin open the big maps and choose the two that depicted both School Hill and the former Ballinger place, later owned by the late Prudhomme. They held the maps against the stable wall while they discussed them.

No, there was no well-defined wagon road between the two places. But there were cow trails that had become roads of a sort. In good weather, a man could get through by daylight with a loaded wagon. Even in the dark, in the snow, two files of men could make good time on the two wheel ruts. He borrowed a soft-lead pencil to sketch in the routes between the Ballinger-Prudhomme place and the town.

"If they don't hit us by noon tomorrow, we'll go after them. If they strike, and any of them get away, we'll go after them. This is where they'll hole up, especially if any of them takes a case of lead poisoning. We're going to wipe this outfit out this time, if we have to pull them out of their hole like a badger," he said.

The boys liked that kind of talk. Meade Hutton showed Hewitt the names of the men he had chosen for duty tonight. Hewitt caught Gavin's eye, and saw that he approved. The one thing that surprised Hewitt was that Meade had picked Albrecht Raue to wait inside Porter Lansing's bank.

"This will be headquarters, Mr. Hewitt. Howard Junkins said he'd stay at the jail all night. I figgered I'd straw-boss around outside and let you stay in command here. There's a fire bell at the depot. It's just louder than hell, and if I see anything of these bastards riding into town, I'll swing on that rope and you bring the boys a-helling," Meade said.

"Good enough, but it's going to be cold and wet out there."

"I growed up in worse country than this. I ain't a baby, Mr. Hewitt."

There was still an undertone of resentment in his voice, but he was, Hewitt thought, entitled to it. Hutton turned up his collar, buttoned his sheepskin coat, and went out into the storm. Hewitt gave the keys to the Farmers and Merchants Bank to Art Gavin, who took Albrecht Raue and a middle-aged cowboy by the name of Skinny Pettit to their duty there. Hewitt himself took two others—Bob Shaeffer and Ike Izaak—to the American Eagle Bank.

He showed the two where to sit, warned them against letting glowing cigarettes show, and locked them inside. The nagging worry that had never quite left his mind came back as he hurried toward the courthouse. There had been a little wind when he first left Mystic's house, and there would probably be more before morning. But for the present, it was as calm as it could be. The heavy snowfall came straight down, blindingly, and rapidly filled every treacherous pothole in the street.

Hewitt smiled to himself. I would hate, he thought, to try to lead a getaway through this stuff by this time tomorrow. . . . A warning thrill shot through him. Jim Sweetland surely would be thinking the same thing. Suddenly it had become highly likely that the old sorehead bandit chieftain would hit tonight, while there was still snow to cover his gang's tracks.

He let himself into the courthouse with the sheriff's key, and opened the door to Gavin's office. He had expected a lamp to be turned down low, but not this total darkness. He jerked his hand out of his coat pocket and thrust it under coat and shirt, to warm it against his bare belly.

Every hair on his body seemed to be tingling. The tingle, in fact, had not stopped since it occurred to him that Sweetland almost *had* to hit tonight. He froze in his tracks, feeling the cold sweat congealing on his face. He held his breath, and in the silence tried to pick up the sounds that would betray someone he knew was there. He had opened the door carelessly, a mistake he should not have made. Whoever it was—

A darker shape came out of the darkness at him, a big

mountain of darkness. He leaned out of the way as much as he could and heard the thud and slam as the man hit the door. He caught Hewitt glancingly, too, and Hewitt cursed his own stupidity as he reeled and lost his balance and went down to one knee. A big fist caught him on the back of the neck. It did not stun him, but the sheer weight and power of it drove him face down on the floor.

He rolled over on his back and tried to kick out with both feet. He felt his heel dig into flesh and knew it was only a thick, powerful thigh. He tried to keep rolling but the man was down on the floor with him, outweighing Hewitt by at least fifty pounds. Hewitt felt the big hands pulling at his coat. He felt an elbow in his throat and a knee in his crotch.

He went limp briefly and then turned his head and sunk his teeth into flesh to the bone and knew he had the man by the wrist. The man gave a deep cry of pain and flinched backward. Hewitt hung on with his teeth. A fist slammed into his cheek and he went blank long enough to let go. He felt the man tugging at the .45 he wore in the trick holster just inside his pants. The front sight slipped under a pawl, and the gun had to be turned to draw it.

He needed just a split second of respite, and the man's struggle with the gun gave it to him. Hewitt could make out the heavy head above him by now. He came up hard and felt his skull smash satisfyingly into a face. He felt the momentary shiver in the big body that meant the man was stunned and hurt.

He butted again, got his toes under him, and drove himself against the powerful, bulky body. A pair of arms went around him and he kept going in a somersault, taking the heavier man with him. He groped in midair for the man's crotch with his hand and got his grip.

He twisted, and the man bellowed in agony and chopped at him with both fists. Hewitt got the .45 out and thumbed back the hammer. He took an elbow in his temple and felt his muscles go slack. He slid the .45 across the floor as he felt the big man pull out of his grasp.

They both came to their feet at the same time. Hewitt tucked his chin into his shoulder and went at the cumbersome shape of darkness with both fists pumping at the guts. They closed, and Hewitt saw next to his face the sheen of white hair. He kept chopping away with both fists as the big man locked his arms around him.

It was Whitey Caskie, and Hewitt got to his wind before Whitey could tighten up and squeeze. Whitey let go of him and stumbled toward the door. Hewitt yanked the .38 out of his shoulder holster and fired twice. The cone of orange light blinked twice and then it was dark again, but he heard Whitey groaning and sliding down to the floor and scratching at the door with his fingertips.

Hewitt stepped backward, not quite trusting his legs. He could taste blood and he knew his nose and mouth had been smashed, and he could not remember when it had happened. He shifted the gun to his left hand and found a match with his right.

"You want to try it again, Whitey, I've still got four shots left, and you would be number nine for me. I'm going to light the lamp now. Keep in mind that I'll see you better than you'll see me," he said. He had trouble keeping his voice steady.

He shifted the gun back to his right hand and groped in the dark for the lamp that usually stood on Gavin's desk at night. It was not there, but there was a little stack of papers. He crumpled them into a loose ball, left it on the corner of the desk, and struck a match. He tossed the match in the paper ball as he stepped smartly away.

The paper flared up and showed him Whitey Caskie lying on his stomach against the closed door. It also showed him the lantern that hung on the opposite wall. He crossed the room, got it down, and levered up the globe.

Whitey came up to his feet and opened the door and was gone before he could strike a match. Hewitt set the lantern on the floor and used his hat to sweep the burning paper from the desk. He took time to tread out several burning pieces, and when he got outside, Whitey had vanished into the snowstorm. Nothing was visible five feet away.

Well, Whitey was carrying a couple of .38 slugs and was not going far. Hewitt went back inside, locking the sheriff's office door behind him. He lighted the lantern and went through the office and cellblock swiftly. He found Howard Junkins in the cell that Whitey had occupied. He was on the floor, on his stomach, and when Hewitt turned him over, the limpness in Howard's neck made him a little sick at his stomach.

Somehow, Whitey had got his arms around Howard's head, and twisted. He had snapped the poor devil's neck more efficiently than a hangman's rope. The puzzling thing was that the cell door was unlocked—*and Howard Junkins had not had a key to it!*

The fire bell began clanging, its voice muffled curiously by the snow. It would be Porter Lansing's bank—of that, Hewitt was sure now. A gunshot smashed through the snowscreen, and then another, and then two more, louder than the bell, and closer. Hewitt snatched up his .45 and took time to stuff two shots into the .38 to replace those fired at Whitey. He went out into the snow, taking time to lock the courthouse behind him.

He could not remember a heavier snowfall. The big, fat flakes came down like a white woolen blanket across his face, with another underfoot. His ribs ached, his battered lips and nose burned, and it was small consolation that Whitey Caskie, wherever he was, had at least one bullet in him.

The fire bell at the depot kept clanging, clanging, clanging. Then it stopped and there was a man's hoarse shout of fear, and Hewitt pitched forward as he stepped off a curb in the snow and fell on his knees. He felt the right one's swift slash of pain, where the skin had been torn off in his fight with Whitey, but at least he knew where he was.

This was the corner where he had first met Porter Lansing, when the old man was driving that trotting stallion, O'Malley's Leo. Turn right here. In the middle of the block he would come to the alley where that first murder had occurred—the one Al Raue had been accused of. The bank was next to it, with its one small window in the wooden sheathing that covered the stone masonry of the vault.

Hewitt got up and plodded on, feeling his way with his feet. He saw dimly the wink of three gunshots where the bank should be. The snowfall muffled their roar as well as the flash of the explosions. A man was yelling with a hoarse urgency that had terror in it.

"Get out of here, get the hell out of the way, goddlemighty, I told you that—"

The whole world seemed to light up. Hewitt leaned into the shattering gust and kept his feet. He heard one more hoarse, male shriek as the roar billowed and thundered around him. And he thought, Dynamite, the old fool used dynamite and he's no better at that than he is at anything else. . . . The snowflakes swirled and eddied and a piece of debris fell lightly on his shoulder. It was a section of cedar lap-siding, like that that had covered the stone wall, and it did not hurt. In a few seconds he could hear again, and what he heard was the voice of a man screaming. Over and over, the same wordless scream of pain, and then it stopped.

CHAPTER SIXTEEN

He yanked out the .45 and began running blindly through the snow, hoping that he remembered his footing. A tall, stooped man in dark clothing, wearing a heavy, black beard, loomed up in front of him. Hewitt remembered that silhouette. He had seen it through the fever and darkness that night on the train when they had tried to lynch Albrecht Raue, and if it was not Jim Sweetland, it was one of his gang.

He lifted the .45 over his head and jabbed down with the butt. He felt the solid, satisfying resistance of bone under a peaked hat. The bearded man let out a yell that was as much fright as pain, but he staggered. Hewitt switched hands on the gun, his right diving toward his hip pocket for the sap. He swung it once, at the last split second giving his wrist the snap that doubled the impact.

He got the bearded man somewhere on the skull, and dropped him like a log. He began shouting, "Form up, boys—form up but hold your fire! We don't want to shoot each other. Gavin, Art Gavin—are you around?"

"Right here, Mr. Hewitt," came a voice from no more than a dozen feet away. "Hold your fire, boys! Don't move, anybody, you hear? Everybody that's a special deputy, drop down and hold your fire! Anybody that moves, take him alive if you can."

Gavin sounded calm, he sounded healthy, and he seemed to be enjoying himself. A moment of silence. On his knees, Hewitt began inching toward the bank, holding the .45 in his left hand. The ground was covered by debris, broken glass, pieces of wood and metal, but he thought the masonry wall still stood.

When he got close enough, still on his knees, he saw that the whole front of the bank had been blown away. The roof was on fire—only a small fire, but it would grow. The square, bulky outline of the steel-lined vault loomed up solidly.

"Sheriff!" Hewitt said softly.

"Right here," came the answer from somewhere through the snow. "What'll you have, Mr. Hewitt?"

"I'm going inside. Someone's got to cover me, and drop anybody that fires at me."

Suddenly it seemed that the snowfall was not so heavy. He heard the sheriff grunt, "Wait a minute, damn the luck," and in a moment saw the old man crawling toward him. Hewitt waited on his knees until Gavin was beside him. Gavin got up on his knees, too, and turned to face the street. He did not raise his voice much beyond its normal tone.

"Mr. Hewitt's going into the bank. Anybody fires toward that bank is a dead man. Go ahead, Mr. Hewitt. You're covered."

Hewitt held the .45 in his right hand and hunched forward, a step at a time, using his left hand to help himself along. There was no door left, no front wall at all. The flames were growing larger and brighter in the roof, illuminating the interior where no snow fell.

There was a dead man lying on his face, feet toward the street. Feeling the floor solid under him, Hewitt stood up and faded back toward the vault. The firelight from the roof showed him another body, and a third lay half in, half out of the building at the rear.

"Mr. Gavin," Hewitt called.

"Hyo!" the sheriff replied.

"There are some dead men here. They'll have to be moved before the roof falls in on them. There's a man knocked out near where you saw me. Get the chains on him and then some of you come give me a hand—quick!"

A moment of silence. Then, "What about the rest of this son of a bitching gang, Mr. Hewitt?"

"There is no rest of it. We got them all."

He waited in silence near the vault, watching the flames eat into the leaning wreckage of roof and walls. A wind was singing strongly out of the northwest by now. The snow still fell in big, wet flakes, but that would change fast. They were in for a blizzard.

At last, Art Gavin's calm voice came: "I got your man chained. He'll live to hang. Guess who it is!"

"Jim Sweetland. Now look for Whitey Caskie, dead. He had a bullet or two in him, and I think he ran straight into the dynamite blast."

He heard Gavin calling for lanterns, and saw the dull twinkle of two. He knew when they found Whitey—dead, as Hewitt had expected. In a moment, Gavin came into the fiercely blazing bank, one of the lanterns in his hand.

Hewitt went to meet him. The lantern was now unnecessary, so bright were the flames from the roof. Just inside the door, a man lay on his face. Gavin handed Hewitt the lantern and knelt to turn the body over.

It was Meade Hutton, with a bullet hole in his chest. Gavin lowered the body to the floor again and stood up. "You don't act surprised, Mr. Hewitt."

"No," was all Hewitt said. "I knew he was in with them when I found Howard Junkins dead and Whitey gone. Meade was the only man who could have done it. Mr. Gavin, he put two pretty good men in this bank tonight—

men he had to get rid of—men he didn't want on his trail when daylight came. Yonder is one of them."

He pointed to a body against the masonry wall of the vault. "Skinny Pettit," Gavin murmured. "Where's Al Raue?"

"I don't know. Probably blown clear outside, when that fool's dynamite went off. But look, Mr. Gavin. Here's what Meade didn't expect—Porter Lansing. Meade got him, sure enough. But he drilled Meade before he died. And see—with the gun he thought was Wes Hardin's."

They would never know for sure, because the blast had moved everything. But Hewitt felt sure that old Porter Lansing had been sitting at his desk when Meade came in. Whether the banker had suspected Meade was another thing they could not know. Certainly, he could not have helped seeing Meade's cold-blooded murder of Skinny Pettit.

Lansing had two slugs in him, and neither need have been fatal, even for an old man. "Only then Sweetland tried to dynamite the vault," Hewitt said, "and he was no better at that than he was at anything else. This is where I went wrong, Mr. Gavin. I expected Sweetland to come riding in with a small army. I should have known better. He had only two men, Whitey Caskie and Meade Hutton, waiting here in town. I ought to be kicked from—"

They both heard it, a hoarse, whimpering moan that was louder than the crackle of flames or the roar of the rising wind. The sound came from the tangle of broken lumber at the rear of the bank, behind the spot where Mystic's desk had stood.

There was no need for lanterns here. The fire illuminated the scene perfectly as they knelt and pulled Albrecht Raue carefully out of the wreckage. Gavin got an arm under the brawny youth's neck, and took out his handkerchief to wipe off the bloody face.

"Poor kid, he's lost a lot of blood," he murmured.

Kneeling beside him, Hewitt said, "Mostly from his nose, I think. Concussion can do that. Let's get him out of here."

Behind them, there was a prolonged crackling sound and an increasing shower of sparks, as the remainder of the roof collapsed slowly. Hewitt thrust Gavin aside, and swung Raue up on his shoulder. And if he's hurt internally, he thought, it's just too bad. Anything's better than burning to death. . . .

Gavin cleared the way for them. The last of the roof came down and flames lighted their path as brightly as daylight. Someone cursed loudly and eloquently in front of the ruined bank, where others were carrying out the bodies of the dead. A hundred feet from the fire, Hewitt staggered to a stop and lowered Raue to the ground.

When Gavin held his lantern close to Raue's face, the boy opened his eyes. "Some way, I got blowed up," he said thickly. "You know what, Art? That damn Meade Hutton, he killed Mr. Lansing."

The wiry little sheriff with the mean face was almost weeping. "I know about that, son," he said. "Ain't nothing to worry about now. Mr. Hewitt, he's done rode this case to a standstill."

It was three-thirty in the morning before Hewitt finished composing his wire to his partner, Conrad Meuse, reporting the end of the case. The two most important bits of information were that Albrecht Raue was cleared of all charges, and that the American Eagle Bank would probably inherit all the business of the burned-out Farmers and Merchants Bank.

Not a part of the telegram, but strictly for his own use, to be dropped like a small bomb in front of Conrad when it came time to settle his expense account, was this list of reward moneys he hoped to collect on the case:

Crowinshield reward	$2,500.00
J.I.B.C. fee	500.00
J.I.B.C. expenses	258.75
American Eagle Bank fee	1,000.00
Burlington rewards	1,000.00
Burlington expenses	303.61
TOTAL	$5,562.36
LESS:	
One-fourth Crowinshield reward to Al Raue	625.00
SUBTOTAL	$4,937.36
LESS:	
Probable reduction in expenses	150.00
FINAL TOTAL	$4,787.36

Art Gavin refused to accept any part of the Crowinshield reward. Jersey Interstate Bonding Corporation would scream at the idea of paying a five-hundred-dollar fee, but Conrad would know how to deal with that. The Burlington, likewise, would not be enamored of the idea of paying a thousand dollars out in rewards, but it had lost a boxcar by burning and a valued detective by murder. In the end, the railroad would pay.

Both J.I.B.C. and the Burlington would want an accounting of the amounts for expenses, which Hewitt had plucked out of thin air. You gave in a little on expenses, to keep their minds off the main bill. And if Conrad was the expert when it came to negotiating fees and rewards, Hewitt took a back seat to no one in negotiating expenses.

It was one of the least satisfactory cases Hewitt had ever worked, from one point of view. He reproached himself for being tardy in sizing up the factors that pointed to Jim

Sweetland as the blundering leadership genius behind the State Line Gang, and it was no excuse to say that he had come into the case late. That was his job, to come in when others had failed. Of course, it was the first time he had ever tried to work a case while running a fever of 104 degrees, but that could not be allowed to set a precedent, either.

In the jail behind the office, Jim Sweetland slept the sleep of exhaustion, with the end of a heavy, six-foot chain padlocked around his ankle. Art Gavin had curled up on the table in the corner of the office, where like the old soldier and cowboy he had been, he slept as comfortably as he would have in a bed.

The one pleasing aspect of the whole case, to Hewitt, was that what had started out as an act of generosity to a boy in trouble had ended in a nice profit to Bankers Bonding & Indemnity Company. Working for pure justice was fine, just fine. But you couldn't beat a profit and loss statement that endorsed the side of the angels, either.

The door opened, and Beth Durant came in, covered with snow. She held the door open for Mystic McDonald, who carried a big, snow-covered basket. The howl of the blizzard outside, and the sudden influx of cold air into the room, awakened Sheriff Art Gavin. He sat up and blinked, trying to figure out where he was, and why.

"Everyone forgets that good hearts beat next to well-filled stomachs," Mystic said, in that soft, clear voice of hers, "so Beth and I brought a few things for tired men to eat."

"I do declare!" said Gavin. "That's thoughtful of you, Mystic. I knowed I was hungry even in my sleep."

Mystic put the basket down on the desk, brushed off the snow, and removed the thick, folded tablecloth that covered fried chicken, sandwiches made of fresh bread, country butter and homemade jam, and a two-quart jug of hot cocoa. A smaller, covered basket, inside the big one, exuded the hot, cinnamony scent of fresh apple turnovers.

"Of course it's not just goodness of heart," Beth said. "We hope we can persuade Mr. Hewitt to stay here in School Hill."

"Been trying to talk him into it myself," Gavin said. "I'm ready to hang up my guns. Ain't nobody going to beat him in an election for sheriff around here—not after today."

He took chicken and a sandwich and began eating. Hewitt got three tincups off the shelf and rinsed them at the water-bucket. He put them down for Beth to fill with cocoa.

"Three?" she said.

"We've got a prisoner to feed," he said, smiling. "I hope you have no objection?"

Neither woman objected. He took food and a cup of cocoa back to Jim Sweetland, who lay on his back on his bunk, star-ing at the ceiling. He gave no sign that he had heard or seen Hewitt.

"Here's some warm food, about the best you could find anywhere, Sweetland. Come over here and get it, because I'm sure not opening your door to serve you," said Hewitt.

"I ain't hungry," replied the prisoner.

"You will be, and you're not going to get food like this. Come on, get up off your hind end and take it."

Sweetland stood up lithely and crossed the cell, ignoring the clank of the chain he dragged behind him. He had the burning eyes of a zealot, full of contempt and fury. He would go to the gallows believing life had cheated him, and that lesser men were killing him out of jealousy.

He took first the food and then the hot cocoa, returned to his bunk without a word of thanks, and began eating. Hewitt turned his back and went back to the office. There had been a time when he could feel pity for even the worst of men, once they were caged and facing execution of a just death sentence. Life had since taught him to save his pity for their victims.

"Of course," Mystic was saying, as he came back and closed the door of the office, "we've been plotting for something other than the sheriff's job for Jeff. I'm almost sure the board of the Farmers and Merchants Bank will offer him the job of president and manager."

The time to stop this was right now. "Not a chance, Mystic," Hewitt said. "There is no Farmers and Merchants Bank any more. Porter Lansing was the bank—the bank was Porter Lansing. His son couldn't possibly handle the job."

"Not even with my help?" she asked.

"Not even with your help. The best thing the board can do is merge with American Eagle, on the best terms it can get, as early as it can get them."

"You mean that there is room for only one bank in School Hill."

"Right now there is. If you could wait—if you could just keep things in suspension for a year or two—but you know the banking laws better than I do. Either the bank opens somewhere within the next few days, or it will remain closed until it is liquidated or merged with another bank."

Her face was impassive, but her downcast eyes gave her away, at least to Hewitt. He understood her, he thought. The power and responsibility she had had in Porter Lansing's bank had meant a lot to her. She had done a good job in guiding a very difficult old man, and now it was over. So was her dream of picking a new banker and guiding him the same way.

"Do you really think Otto Groshardt is a good enough banker to do the job?" she said, raising her eyes at last.

"I do. He's still green about some things, and he'll need advice. I hope you'll work with him as you did Porter Lansing."

"Oh, he wouldn't want my advice!" she said, but her pleading eyes told a different story.

"Wait and see," was all he said. But it was one more thing he had to do before leaving School Hill—see the stubborn old German banker, and make him understand how lucky he would be to have Mystic at his elbow.

"So it's another case closed," Beth Durant said.

"Yes."

"Where will you go from here?"

"Depends on what I hear from my partner. I'll wire him as soon as the depot is open, and wait for his reply. If there is no other case, I'll go back to Cheyenne and get acquainted with my own office again."

"And if there is a case?" This time, there was a definite break in her voice.

"Well, in my business, you can't wait for the work to come to you. You go where the work is."

Silence a moment. Then Mystic said what Beth wanted to say and could not: "Doesn't all that travel get to be terribly boring and tiresome, though?"

He looked her straight in the eye. "Oh, perhaps it does now and then, but by nature, I reckon, I'm a traveling man."